THE SACRED HOOP

D1507138

The Sacred Hoop

BILL BRODER

SIERRA CLUB BOOKS

SAN FRANCISCO

FOR MY MOTHER AND FATHER
CELIA M. BRODER AND HYMAN C. BRODER

The Sierra Club, founded in 1892 by John Muir, has devoted itself
to the study and protection of the earth's scenic and ecological resources—
mountains, wetlands, woodlands, wild shores and rivers, deserts and plains.
The publishing program of the Sierra Club offers books to the public
as a nonprofit educational service in the hope that they may enlarge
the public's understanding of the Club's basic concerns.
The point of view expressed in each book, however, does not necessarily represent
that of the Club. The Sierra Club has some sixty chapters coast to coast,
in Canada, Hawaii, and Alaska. For information about how you may participate
in its programs to preserve wilderness and the quality of life,
please address inquiries to Sierra Club, 730 Polk Street,
San Francisco, CA 94109.

Copyright © 1979 by Bill Broder
Sierra Club Books paperback edition: 1992

All rights reserved under International and Pan-American Copyright Conventions.
No part of this book may be reproduced in any form or by any electronic or
mechanical means, including information storage and retrieval systems,
without permission in writing from the publisher.

LIBRARY OF CONGRESS CATALOGING IN PUBLICATION DATA
Broder, Bill, 1931-
The sacred hoop : a cycle of earth tales / Bill Broder.
p.   cm.
ISBN 0-87156-583-8
1. Philosophy of nature—Fiction.   2. Man—Influence on nature—
History—Fiction.   I. Title.
PS3552.R619S2   1992   813'.54—dc20   91-33694
CIP

Production by Amy Evans
Cover design by David Bullen

This book was designed by James Robertson and Diana Fairbanks at
The Yolla Bolly Press, Covelo, California. The text was set in Monotype Bembo at
Mackenzie-Harris Corporation, San Francisco. Titles were set by hand in
Caslon 545 and Caslon 471 at The Yolla Bolly Press. The book was printed and bound
by the Courier Companies, Inc., Westford, Massachusetts.

Printed in the United States on acid-free paper containing a minimum of 50% recovered waste
paper, of which at least 10% of the fiber content is post-consumer waste
10 9 8 7 6 5 4 3 2 1

Contents

The End of the Beginning

All of the tales in this book rest upon archaeological or historical evidence. A number of the characters unquestionably lived: Lu-igisa, in fact, did write to his mistress Arnabtum in Sumeria; Huldah no doubt prophesied in the second quarter of Jerusalem; King Desiderius found his capital city, Pavia, besieged by Charlemagne's army; the friendship of Rothkav, Egbert, and Wendilo was chronicled by responsible sources; and the mother of a renowned astronomer survived a witch's trial in southern Germany. However, *The Sacred Hoop* is fiction, each story shaped according to my purpose or concerns. I have wanted to show the changing relationship of humankind to earth in the Western world. This relationship has been complicated by our membership in communities and our worship of gods. I have therefore attempted to place my characters in situations pertinent to these problems rather than to approximate some truth about them as they actually existed.

"Relationship to earth" is a resounding phrase, but for me the words call to mind a vacant lot on the corner of Lawrence and LaSalle, next door to my childhood house in the middle of the city of Detroit. I called the lot—filled with trees and trails and small hilly mounds—"the woods." To a small child these woods seemed vast and varied. A large oak stood at the center; a good-sized elm intruded upon the sidewalk, which had been cut to accommodate it. A number of lesser trees grew limbs low enough for me to climb even before I started school. The mounds were good for sledding in the winter; ditches were easily converted to defensible bastions in trench and Indian warfare. Squirrels, robins, ants, rats from the alley, grasshoppers, sparrows, chipmunks, and local cats and dogs represented nature's bounty. And there were sudden summer thunderstorms to remind me of nature's power.

Later I could not believe how small a section of earth these woods took up—the space for one small house which was built there. But size did not matter. In that vacant lot I felt dirt, hard and grainy, soft and malleable; I experienced the density of stone, the coarseness of bark, and the sensual veininess of the undersides of leaves.

I did not learn the proper names of any of those natural creatures I encountered as a child, nor much about their lives. My people all but ignored nature, except to thank God for its bounties. Even though my great-grandparents in the Old World sold fishing lines, hooks, and nets, and lived under the same roof as their goats and cows, their attention was focused on such questions as: "How should we treat one another under the constant gaze of a vigilant God?" and "What are our duties to one another and to that God?" I think the most they asked of animals was whether their hooves were cloven, or how best to slit their throats and salt their flesh so that God would not be offended. If the Jews of the Lithuanian Confederacy had any feeling for animals or nature, it was all but lost by the time my great-uncle reached Detroit and sent for the rest of the family. It seemed almost as if the covenant which had made them a people devoted to justice and morality had excluded them from nature.

In my childhood, nature resided in that vacant lot next door. It was another room of the house which I loved. I spent a great deal of time at the window sitting on the radiator looking out, pondering the justices and injustices of family life. It made no difference which side of the window I found myself—it was all one. The people and the moral problems which occupied my consciousness inside the house accompanied me on my solitary picnics in the crotch of the roots of the great oak in the middle of my woods. Then the woods were populated by the spirits of the living. Later, the spirits of the dead, often more powerful, would join them.

I was born into the nature of that small lot, as well as into a tribe involved primarily in getting along with one another and into a nation concerned with getting ahead. In my earliest years, I grew to believe that nature, the Good, and God were part of a single satisfying whole of which I was a part. When I reached adolescence, I found myself estranged from the Good and God. The command, "Be good!" came clearly, day in and day out. Too often it seemed to have more to do with correct dress, manners, and success than it did with the proper goal of life. The community, representative of "the many hoops" of which Black Elk spoke at the beginning of this book, appeared to want shined shoes, a proper haircut, and the esteem of others more than it wanted a virtuous life. God seemed to be absent from all the rituals within which His name was uttered and deliberately I sought out only the hypocrisy rather than any trace of true feeling. Because I found the community oppressive and hypocritical, I fled it. Nature provided refuge: first the woods next door, and later the deserted beaches of Lake Michigan and the reaches of the Namakogan and St. Croix rivers of northern Wisconsin. By using nature as a refuge, I did it little honor; and, in return, the comfort nature afforded proved to be fleeting.

By the time I left Detroit, my father had died and I was most concerned with the meaning of the word "good" which had given me so much trouble in my youth. I studied philosophy, hoping to find in that discipline an answer to my questions. One sunny afternoon, a middle-aged man in a tweed jacket with elbow patches leaned up against a green blackboard and jauntily brought a piece of chalk up towards his lips as if it were a cigarette—smoking was prohibited—conveying to me the idea that the Good and the multitude of commandments over which it presided rested upon an arbitrary decision for which there was no reason, no prior law, no revelation. I had discussed these ideas before; I had argued them and even pondered them, but for some reason on this particular afternoon I experienced the truth that no matter how far back you pursue the Good you will finally have to come to some moment when you merely agree to believe in it—for no good reason other than that you need a firm foundation upon which to build your moral world. I was furious at that professor, although he spoke in the innocence of pedantry. I think that I expected him to say that if I pursued the Good back far enough, I would find my dead father, his hair thinning and graying, his thick black brows bushing over the pure steel of his glasses, and his large brown eyes, both kindly and stern, promising the joys and the responsibilities of goodness. The teacher was not exactly saying that my father had never existed, merely that my father's beliefs rested on an arbitrary decision which no one ever admitted. I was not at all happy with this new knowledge. Indeed, I felt that philosophy had shown itself bankrupt by offering me such ideas as truths.

The events of the modern world had served to undermine any hope that civilization would progress towards a peaceful moral state. The twentieth century had labored mightily and had managed to bring forth horror: wars, genocide, the breakdown of world organizations, and the rebirth of passionate ethnic exclusiveness all over the planet. Neither God nor the Good appeared to have any relevance to this destructive working out of historical anarchy, and everyone treated nature as an inexhaustible supply depot. And yet, all over the world, individual human beings continued to believe in the struggle to live with one another and with earth in peaceful harmony. I wished to be a part of this struggle. God, nature, and the Good, born in me at my most impressionable age, remained living concepts. The unity which had joined them in my childhood, and which would have guided me, now proved elusive.

Although it took many years before I grew into an awareness of how I might approach my goal, one event marked a beginning. A close friend had been introduced to a campsite on a granite outcropping over the rapids of a Sierra river by an eighty-year-old man he met on the trail. Generously, my friend shared this magnificent gift with me. One morning I noticed a peculiar bird hopping comically about the stones of the rapids. Its eccentric motions and the gorgeous song which came from its throat filled me with joy. I asked the bird's name and was told it was an ouzel, one of John Muir's favorite birds. Muir had once called the ouzel "an outgrowth of the streams themselves, derived from them like flowers from the ground, as if the pebbles around which the waters had sung for ages had at length been overgrown with feathers and flown away." That day I felt as if I had returned to the innocence which I had experienced in the woods of the vacant lot on Lawrence Avenue. It seemed to me that if I learned more about the ouzel, and the stream, and the granite through which it had cut, I would find myself nearer to the goal for which I had been searching.

For the first time in my life, I began to learn the names of living beings other than humans. I started late, and often forgot my lessons. But a wonder grew within me at the way in which life had managed to begin on this planet and had survived. The theory of evolution in its modern forms amazed and delighted me by its elegant simplicity. Many of the philosophic problems which I had puzzled as a youth appeared to yield to natural theories which began at the beginning. Another friend took me out into the California countryside to experience the yearly miracle of wildflowers, many of which he grew in his own back yard. Only a few of the names he taught me remained from year to year, but those few and the life they identified brought me into an even more intimate contact with the spirit of earth which I sought. A third friend asked me to help him put words to his vision of a human advocacy for the natural world; through this task I learned about cycles and systems and natural balance. Gradually a sense of the coherence of life took root within me, a coherence in which human beings had a place. Now I began to understand how God could exist. By what better name could one call the way in which everything fits together?

Another morning in the Sierras I climbed down the great boulders to a deep channel below a roaring granite chute. I slipped into the azure water and let the current carry me downstream to a gentle beach. When I emerged, a warm full breeze dried me. I sat for some hours on the sun-warmed granite. Returning to my friends at camp, I felt that the voyage into a full life presided over by nature, the Good, and God, which had been interrupted by my departure from my "woods" and by my father's death, had been resumed. My father, who had seldom stepped off of a sidewalk during his entire life, stood there beside me in the Sierra along with all other human beings, alive or dead. The wilderness existed not as an empty refuge, but as a generator of all life, including human life and consciousness.

I went back to my reading in history, philosophy, anthropology, and biology. I began to understand that the covenant by which the Good arose was not nearly so arbitrary as I had thought. The hoop of life and the hoop of peoples formed a continuous whole. Just as my personal wilderness in the vacant lot next door to my childhood house and the Sierra canyon of my later years were peopled with the human community in which I lived, so the wilderness of earth necessarily includes "people in their multitude." Nor can the multitude continue to stand "apart from the trees, unraveling in their hearts a scheme about pain." Human beings have been given the gift of understanding and the power of choice by nature. Their decisions now determine the fate of life on earth. They cannot continue to consider history and nature as separate. *The Sacred Hoop* begins with the statement that there was no beginning; it is my hope that there will be no ending.

. . . the universe is alive, has soul in it,
and is full of gods.

THALES

And I saw that the sacred hoop of my people was one
of many hoops that made one circle, wide as daylight
and as starlight, and in the center grew one mighty
flowering tree to shelter all the children of one
mother and one father. And I saw it was holy.

BLACK ELK

Then the first wind touched God's eyes
and He saw it in a cloud of glory,
and thought It is good. *He didn't think then*
about people, people in their multitude.
But they already were standing apart from the trees,
unraveling in their hearts
a scheme about pain.

NATAN SACH

The Hoop Is Planted

I

A Beginning

In the beginning there was no beginning, only an emptiness in the midst of which quivered a black egg full of very small things. And then, the egg exploded, breaking the small things into even smaller things and hurling them out into the lonely void where they rushed about seeking each other's comfort. Wherever they found mates, they united, and then united again. Here, then here, and then here, billions of small things collapsed together into clusters, larger and larger, forming the first generation of stars.

Our own galaxy formed, rotating slowly in the immense emptiness called the universe. Clouds of gas and dust swirled about the new stars. One particular cloud began to thicken, rotating around a center. The faster the small things moved towards the center, the hotter they became. They stuck together with such force that they fused, releasing great power out into space. This particular cloud had become our sun.

Still there remained a good deal of swirling gas and dust which the sun had not swallowed. Pockets began to form among these small things—clusters influenced by the sun, rotating around it. Soon nine satellites to our sun formed, the wandering ones, the planets. The third satellite in distance from our sun we call earth, the ground on which we stand, out of which we have grown. But when all this happened, there were no names for these things, no "stars," no "galaxies," no "sun," and no "earth." The givers of these names had not yet arrived.

Today when we tell the story of the beginning of the universe, the solar system, earth, life and humankind we do not speak of gods full of love or anger. Instead we credit laws according to which small things attract one another, rotate and gather into clusters which collapse and explode. We talk of fusion and fission, of elements, of variation, selection and evolution. We attempt to avoid mentioning a purpose to these events. Everything happens because . . . it happens, and it is the happening which we are supposed to worship.

Nevertheless we are believers. An element of the sacred edges into every account of our origins. The words, once spoken, evoke an echo in our feelings and we become full of awe. Through the ages we have worshipped at many shrines. Each altar has faced towards a different god, taking on the shape of our separate hazardous histories. Only earth has remained and its three miracles: that things exist at all, that life came out of things, and finally, that life became conscious of itself.

Our church is everywhere, for that is where we find our miracles. The way we understand matter, life and consciousness, and the respect we pay them, determine all of our acts. We plant grain, we harvest it, mill it, sell and buy it, knead, bake, serve and eat it according to the way in which we understand the meaning of stone, tree and child. When we have recognized these miracles and have been able to organize a proper worship of them, there may come a hope for the future.

Among the particles of gas and dust which clustered together to form our planet, and within the clumps of matter which bombarded its surface lay hidden the makings of a whole new order of being. As earth cooled, the clouds surrounding it condensed, raining water down upon its uneven surface. Oceans formed amidst dry land. By chance, an unyielding force kept the planet orbiting around the sun at just the correct distance from the source of heat and energy that the oceans remained liquid: nearer, the water would have dried up; further off, it would have frozen. The water which lay in the seas provided a nourishing home in which the new order of being could develop. Energy flowing from the sun fueled the process. Water coursed over the planet, carrying matter here and there in varying proportions, yielding an endless variety of wet and dry. Matter began to combine with itself in a way which would not stop, progressing to new matter in a chain reaction which wedded matter and fire, along with water and wind into a single ongoing system—delicate and tough, evanescent and enduring —which human beings later called life.

[18]

Eventually, living matter created an atmosphere in which it could flourish. A magnificent array of life forms developed upon our planet: some floating in the seas or rooted to the ground, others flying about the lower reaches of the air, and still others crawling about the surface of earth. Great forests of trees grew up to cover dry land. Nourished by the sun's heat and deluges of rain, these trees provided an hospitable refuge for second and third layers of life—birds and insects and all sorts of mammals. Among the mammals in the trees, a long-tailed, rodent-shaped creature with thirty-four teeth, an opposable thumb and binocular vision proved to be so successful that it gave birth to a variety of creatures which still survive upon earth: monkeys, baboons, apes and apelike creatures who would evolve into the ancestors of human beings.

And then the forests began to shrink. Some slight tilt of the poles, a flare on the corona of the sun, a minute variation in orbit caused a change in climate. Droughts which lasted many years scorched the trees; early frosts ravaged young buds; volcanos and lightning storms ignited fires that consumed wide swaths of the vulnerable plants. Many of the weakest trees succumbed to insects and disease. Thus the creatures who before had been graciously housed in the forests, living in a happy equilibrium with the creatures around them, found themselves crowded together. Aloft amidst the delicious acorn and the luscious fruit which could be picked at will, there commenced a battle for survival.

The strongest and most agile remained in the trees. Others, our apelike ancestors among them, came to the ground, seeking nourishment increasingly in the open savannas. In order to survive, our ancestor began to walk upright, to manipulate tools and weapons with its hands, to hunt in groups, to communicate with sounds, to band together in families and tribes, and to use its mind in order to dominate the system of life into which it had been born.

II

Out of the Garden

NIGHT has fallen. Being careful to keep upwind of his prey, Dag makes his way down from the canyon's rim where he has been hiding. For days he has stalked them; no easy task. While they are not intelligent, they are sensitive to smell and sound. Of all hunting, he dislikes this the most. It's ironic that in his old age he should pick up his weapons for this prey. Sometimes he relives these hunts in his dreams, compressing ten days into a few minutes. Always, just as he is delivering the fatal blow, he recognizes himself as the victim. He wakes sweating and groaning, and Etana gathers him to her bosom. After such a dream, he has to be comforted for hours. He wishes that his kind could think of some way to share the South Hills, the River Plains, and the High Mountains with this other creature as they do with the rest of the animals. But, as Etana keeps assuring him, this other is different.

Etana presents these matters in terms of survival. She assures him that she regrets such necessities as much as he does. She carries on these discussions in a quiet, logical, yet passionate manner. When he balks, as he often does, she cheerfully goes about her business. She never displays contempt or rancor, although he believes she is further of sight and quicker of understanding than he is—than all of them.

As a young man, he often wished he had married a girl of his own clan. Their customs forbade it. Marriage had brought great alliances, new tools, and knowledge. The spear launcher, which gave the hunter an immense added thrust, had come to them by marriage; so had the feathered arrow, and the bow-operated fire drill. None of these new ways, however, had changed their feeling for earth. They had not lost their wonder and respect for the life-force which worked through spirits, nor for the gods which filled all things. They had viewed their simplest acts—eating, hunting, making love, voiding—as part of a re-creation of the world. The names of animals and plants by which they ordered their affairs had displayed their easy familiarity with the life of the land, the waters and the sky.

But change has come to their lives. He knows it is wrong to put the blame on Etana. She did not create the famines, the droughts, the dis-appearing herds, the struggle with these other creatures who threaten their permanent home. Etana has brought him and his people great power to solve their problems. With her knowledge, Etana has eased the way for change.

∵

Dag splits the attack force into three units. Once again he has taken the assignment on the up-canyon side. He is a wise commander who does not risk his people out of false bravery. Etana had suggested that he remain in the village: this hunt, she said, was a young man's affair. He had replied that the responsibility for the crime would have to be shared by them all, but particularly by him, the first among equals. At the word "crime" she had smiled and had gone about her work.

From his vantage point, he is obliged to watch these others half the night. He finds this the most distressing time of all—seeing them go about their routine which is not all that different from his own. After two days he has gotten to know them: the three big families, the old ones, the newly mated pair, and all the lively young. At moments, he feels such a yearning that he wants to run down, shouting and laughing, and embrace them. After all, he has scarcely met any of his own kind during his lifetime. The world seems a very empty place. And then here are these creatures, like him in so many ways. He wishes they had not chosen to wander so close to the birthplace of the Seed Mother.

Although he cannot mention this to anyone, he believes that it is the Seed Mother who drives him to commit this crime. He will never feel comfortable praying to this new goddess who has usurped the power of the Animal Goddess, "She who lives in the ice caves of the north."

[22]

But then, for generations his people have been feeling uneasy about the Animal Goddess. As a child, Dag had often heard the old ones tell of the great fire drives of the past by which human beings had offended that icy goddess, the Tree Spirit, and the God of Fire. He had listened in terror to the vivid descriptions of the burning forests and meadows. In his dreams he had heard the piteous cries of the thick-hided beasts as they tumbled over the rimrock attempting to flee the flames. He had awakened cringing at the vision of the untouched carcasses of the dead, their eyes glazed in fear, their flesh rotting in full view of the gods. The old ones claimed that the destruction of so much life to fill the small needs of the people had caused the gods to retreat from their familiar groves, pools, and caves to distant sanctuaries where they looked down upon human activities with suspicion. Dag's own grandfather said that he had seen the land of the great beasts in the north change from almost unbroken forests to great rolling grassy plains, all because of the fires. He had often warned of a great retribution to come. Dag had laughed at the old man, claiming that the grass nourished a wonderful new and full life, but recently, in his own old age, Dag had come to wonder whether his kind had a right to change the earth so significantly.

∵

Down below, the others are going about their business peacefully. Filled with remorse, he contemplates calling off the attack. When they work with their hands, however, his resolve returns. He doesn't know why the hands set him off so. They seem to stand for everything else which is inferior and threatening about these creatures. His own kind, either right-handed or left-handed, are good with their hands. These others favor neither hand, and seem to get confused when a task requires the coordination of both hands. He becomes furious when he sees them trying to shape a chopper, knocking first with one stone and then with the other, as if they were backward children trying to make two tools at the same time. He wants to shake them. Then there is that large jaw of theirs, with the enormous teeth. Their eating disgusts him. The noises they make to one another disturb him also. They communicate, and he can recognize their emotions, but the sounds frighten him, almost as if animals had been given the impulse to speak.

[23]

He would much prefer to be stalking animals. His kind worships animals. Animals give life. Animals watch over his band; they were the first ancestors; and if animals are treated well, they offer themselves up for the hunt, providing food, clothing, and even tools. These creatures, on the other hand, seem useless as prey. No one would want one of their hides, nor would their flesh make very good eating. It's as if the gods had set forth a strange image of humans to confuse his people, to frighten their game away, and to take the very food out of their mouths.

Dag tries to whip up his anger for that moment when he will strike. Still he blames the Seed Mother, for it is she whom he is protecting; it is she who has supplanted the animals. Without her bounty, his people would never have settled permanently in this place which now requires defending.

∵

The people had settled on the hilltop at the bend of the river only a few generations before Dag was born. The stories he heard as a child clearly reflected an uncertainty about the new way of life in this place and a yearning for the past. The stories told how the people had come to depend so greatly upon grain.

When they had come upon this site, they had been a nomadic tribe of hunters and gatherers, following the large game. At first the hilltop had seemed like any other campsite, a trifle richer perhaps, and more comfortable. On the wooded hills, familiar grasses grew which fed the large hooved animals. Oak, pistachio, and almond freely gave up their fruit. Wild sheep, goats, cattle, and pigs thrived, providing meat. And, almost as a gift, on the steep slopes of the mountains, great fields of a new sort of wild grass offered up a bounty of seeds which the women gathered with little effort. They had never found a richer place before, and they remained a good deal longer than they had intended. After a while, several neighboring clans, their hunting partners from the north, joined them. It seemed odd at first to be living together for such a long time without moving, but the countryside was bountiful, and before long they became accustomed to remaining in one place.

One day the people realized that their numbers had nearly tripled. The care with which they kept the campsite saved them from murderous illnesses. Old people remained with them for many more years than before; infants managed to survive the early months in greater numbers. To feed so many mouths, the hunters had to travel for weeks away from the camp. Now the young men spoke up, saying they would all starve if they remained at the bend of the river. But the people had lost their taste for moving about. They pointed out that there was more than enough to eat without large game: turtles, land snails, fish, fresh-water crabs, shellfish, partridges, and even water birds which visited spring and fall; fruits, nuts and roots, also, and, of course, the seeds of the tall wild grass which sprang up miraculously year after year. More and more, the people had become entranced by the wild grass and its seeds which could be prepared in so many different ways.

And so, their diet changing, they remained on the hilltop at the bend of the river, turning more and more to the wild grass for sustenance. At first this plant was not quite suited to the people's habits. When the seeds were just ripe enough for eating, they were also very loosely attached to their mother plant. At the slightest touch or a breath of the wind, the seed broke off, fell, and was lost to the gatherer. The plant had evolved this ability to cast off its ripe seeds in order to survive.

Of course, like all other living creatures, the seed of the wild grass was never the exact replica of the mother plant. Now and then plants grew husks which did not shatter even when the wind blew its hardest. Naturally, the people of the clans managed to retrieve more of these odd, nonshattering varieties of wild grass than the others. Many of the seeds they gathered fell upon the ground around their camp where bare disturbed soil was in great abundance: paths, old dumps, and fireplaces. Thus the nonshattering variety of the grassy plant grew up in abundance in and around the campsite. Slowly the people began to understand that they had been blessed with a permanent food source which they could trust.

The old ones who told these stories did not approve of the partnership which had grown up between the new variety of wild grass and the people. They pointed out that the new type of plant upon which they had come to depend had given up its ability to get its own seed into the ground unaided; unless human beings guaranteed the seed a fair planting, the nonshattering plant would not survive. Wherever the people abandoned the plant, it perished, and the soil, which it had held to the surface of the earth, blew away. In the joy of their discovery of a domestic plant, the people did not notice the slow but sure disappearance of the wild plant on the mountainside. Once again, the old ones explained, the gods were displeased with humans for meddling with life on earth. But the gods continued to forgive and protect them.

In order to store and grind the seeds of the new plant, the people began to make heavy vessels from the mud of the river bottom. Soon, a mud house was built, and with it came a time of disputes. Violent arguments arose over permanent homesites, especially between families of different clans. One day, the wife of one of the clan leaders picked up a sharp-pointed stick and began to draw a map on the flat earth next to the main fire. Everyone forgot his anger and crowded around, attempting to see the image she drew. There before them was the home camp, with every tree and rock outcrop plainly marked. To everyone's amazement, the map maker now began to divide the map into separate plots, using a series of grid lines. Where, they wondered, did those lines come from? There was nothing like them to be seen around the camp. And what did they mean? The hunters and their families began to shift about from one foot to another, longing to leave. When the woman had finished, she rose and explained that they would draw lots for each of the squares on the map. The family who chose a square could build a house there. That square would be theirs, and theirs alone.

In bewilderment, the hunters and their wives and their children sat down in the dust. Never before had they come across a place which belonged to them alone. Every place belonged to all creatures. Even the hearth back in their old territory had been used by other bands when they were off traveling, and whatever was left behind was freely taken up. They shared weapons among themselves, and tools, and the fruits of the hunt. Now, here on the ground, the woman's marks showed a place which each family, and no one else, would own.

The lots were soon drawn and the houses begun. They worked together—the whole camp helping each family to build its house. In this way the new village was completed quickly; a place where the people would remain forever.

Now two words which had seldom been heard among the people became the most popular words in camp: "my" and "mine." And as their language, their housing, their habits of travel, their implements, and their diets changed, so did their prayers. Feeling deserted by the Animal Goddess, they began to worship the Seed Mother and the Sky God who sent down his waters to nourish the grain fields, to keep the rivers flowing and the wells full. They were not sure where these gods lived.

To the old ones and to Dag it seemed as if the gods had receded even farther and now looked down upon humankind with disgust.

∵

Down below, the others are eating raw meat, pulling it apart with their hands and those big teeth of theirs. They have a fire, but they never use it for cooking. That is his meat they are putting into their stomachs. And it will be his grain soon, too, if he doesn't act. Other bands of his own kind respect his territory, and he respects theirs. He hasn't seen much of them recently, but when marriage time comes, there are meetings and exchanges. And they talk together. Dag's kind talks beautifully. The words are like newly sprouted flowers, bright and colorful and comforting. He likes to play with the separate sounds because they can be combined every which way to mean something different each time. Words are his most perfect tools. They fit his mouth like the skin of an animal fits its flesh. Curious and precise, with a passion for order, his kind has named the world—every particular sort of grass, every bush, tree, bird, and beast. They have named even the different kinds of snow that fall in the mountains and the different kinds of snow that lie on the ground. They name things for which they have no use, and others which merely delight them. Some things they name twice and three times. The only words Dag fears and regrets are "my" and "mine."

Dag gives the order to prepare. The second force is about to launch its diversionary attack from the flanks. He must creep down the hillside to bar the cave entrance. The other is larger than his kind, and could easily win in a one-to-one battle, but it never seems to learn tactics. Its reactions are always predictable.

[27]

There! The first missile has been thrown. The shouting commences. He waits for them to turn and chase the decoys. Now he slips down with his companions in front of the cave. He leads his force forward to the backs of this familiar enemy. His well-hafted axe arcs forward to split that illshaped skull of the odd two-legged cousin who must be destroyed so that his own line will flourish. As the blood leaps out and the heavy body falls, his own spirit leaps and falls.

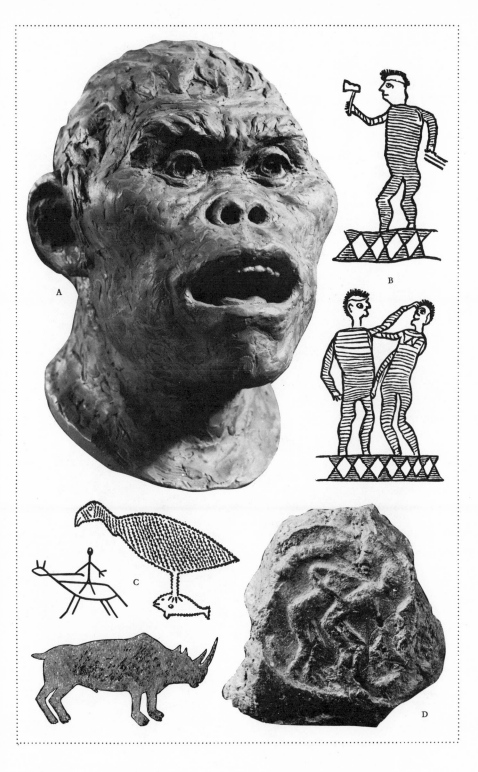

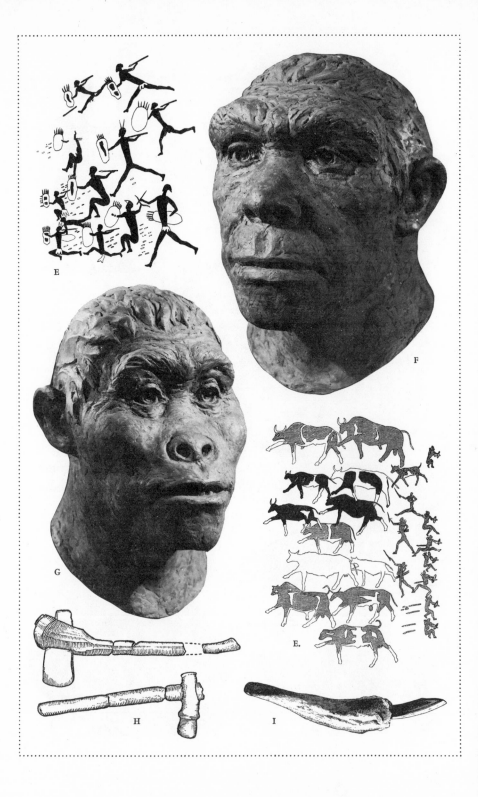

E

F

G

E.

H

I

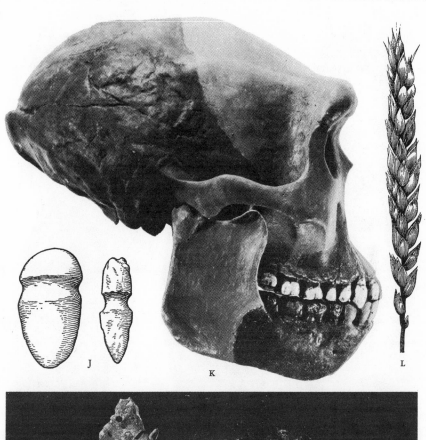

J K L

M

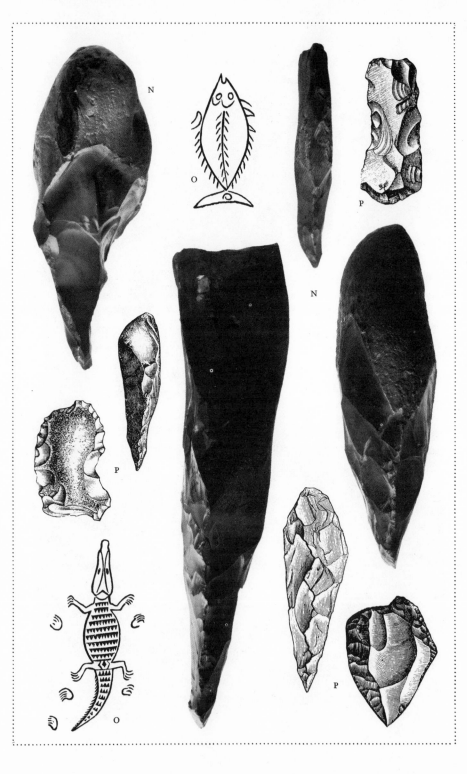

A Ancient man of Africa, *Australopithecus prometheus*, a reconstruction, courtesy of the American Museum of Natural History.

B Art of hunter-gathering people: warriors.

C Art of hunter-gathering people: animals.

D Adam and Eve chased from the Garden, a seal impression, Mesopotamia, reproduced by permission of the University Museum, University of Pennsylvania.

E Hunters of Africa, Bushmen.

F Ancient man of Africa, Rhodesian man, a reconstruction, courtesy of the American Museum of Natural History.

G Ancient man of Africa, *Paranthropus robustus*, a reconstruction, courtesy of the American Museum of Natural History.

H Axe and hammer made of stone and horn.

I Hog's tooth chisel.

J Stone mallets.

K Skull of ancient man of Africa, *Pithecanthropus*, courtesy of the American Museum of Natural History.

L Bald wheat.

M Early Mesopotamian grave objects, reproduced by permission of the University Museum, University of Pennsylvania.

N Chisel-pointed stone instruments of early man, photographs courtesy of the American Museum of Natural History.

O Art of hunter-gathering people: animals.

P Drawings of paleolithic hand axes.

O

III

To Do Earths

ONE spring morning a great mischief was discovered in the Northwestern District of the Larsa Irrigation Administration. A major sluice gate of the Etellum Canal had been jammed open, admitting a vast flood of waters to the feeder canals, ditches and furrows. The lands belonging to Lu-igisa, "Kind-faced Man," Chief Contractor of the district, were particularly affected. In view of the exceptional rains that year, it was feared that many of the neighboring lands would also be flooded unless extraordinary measures were taken to repair the damage.

The local military commandant reported that the waters had invaded the first floor of Lu-igisa's house, leaving everything in great disarray. The Chief Contractor had apparently disappeared, as well as his family. On the sleeping roof of the house investigators found a confusing array of objects: an incense burner, still smoking, a half-filled cup of sacramental wine, several neat piles of irrigation records, stacked in perfect order, and two letters of recent date which read as follows:

From Lu-igisa to Arnabtum, speak. This is what Lu-igisa says: What have I done, that Nur-Sin took my canal away from me and gave it to Thorn-wood? And Thorn-wood has been able to act spitefully towards me, because he gave it to him, threatening to distrain my family for debts incurred in the service of the King. If the canal is silted up because of his woeful neglect, then in court he will surely say that he claimed it legally. If you are my lady, speak to Nur-Sin that he may return my canal to me. But if this does not work out, for any subsequent service he need not ask, and the ruin of the land shall be on his head, and on that of the King. Now send me a reply to this sealed document.

From Arnabtum to Lu-igisa. This is what Arnabtum says: I return your rash letter. Nur-Sin has turned his face from you and I can do no more. What did you expect? I have warned you for years. Now you must pay the price of your negligence. You have guarded your precious canals, but have neglected water for the fertile palms of the capital. You refuse to play according to the hidden rules, to make friends with your surpluses, to take advantage of your debtors, and, worst of all, you publicly criticize royal water policy. You have never been forgiven for your opposition to the Nippur-Isin War. You might have repaired your fortunes if you had come more often to the capital, but instead you have buried yourself in the country, under the silt of floods. You have buried our happiness too.

Lu-igisa, "Kind-faced Man," was a modest administrator who had borne up under many calamities. Early in his career, his beloved first wife and daughter died of the pestilence after they had been taken hostage by the bureaucrats for debts he had inherited from his father. His second family had been swept from him by the Great Flood, and his two eldest sons by a third wife had died in the Nippur-Isin War. But as long as he had his work, the care of his beloved canals, he found consolation. Families, he maintained, were but offspring of the earth and the life-giving waters in his care. The Gods could scourge the land with droughts and floods; they could scourge man with pestilence, injustice and war; but as long as man kept faith with the channels, the dikes, the embankments and the canals, the earth would flower and families would be renewed.

Lu-igisa was proud of his work. For twenty years he had been Chief Contractor of the Northwestern District, directly under the control of the Royal Canal Administrator, Nur-Sin, who reported to King Sumuel himself. As the King always said, quoting the tombs of kings before him, "The canals are the chief glory of the kingdom for from them comes all power of increase." Lu-igisa had grown up in the public works system, priding himself as much on his meticulous records as on the actual dredging and the repair of the dikes. His canals, feeder ditches, dikes and towpaths were the best kept in the land. Under his just patronage, canal workers, overseers, footmen, boatmen, brick carriers, clerks, paymasters, granary operators, inspectors, and migrant workers labored loyally. Despite setbacks, he himself prospered, slowly adding to his own lands. He looked forward to a content and industrious retirement as a private farmer.

[36]

Nor did Lu-igisa neglect to thank the gods. Every year at New Years, in times of grief or joy, he had journeyed to Larsa, the capital, to vow his great belief in the Earth Renewal. At one such celebration early in his career, he had met his mistress, Arnabtum, a lady of the Court and a great favorite of Nur-Sin. Every New Year, hand and hand, he and his cunning mistress mingled with the vast throngs of the city, dancing, drinking and offering up prayers to the Great Sky, the Great Waters, the Great Earth, and the Harvest God. High above them, in the pure white temple perched upon the immense ziggurat, the King, dressed as Tammuz, handsome young God of the Harvest, garlanded with flowers of the nether world, rose from his death bier to marry the High Priestess, dressed as Inanna, Goddess of Love and Fertility. After the hot dry summer, the life-giving waters of the New Year were commencing. During these celebrations, Lu-igisa's passion for Arnabtum and his love of the fertile land and loyalty to the great city which guaranteed the land's flowering, fused into a single joy. He returned to his work on the canals a dedicated man. Arnabtum recognized in Lu-igisa the enduring qualities which had brought greatness to Larsa—energy and ingenuity, devoted orderliness and an earthy kindness and devotion. In the midst of the slippery confusions of the capital, the lovely lady of the Court treasured her yearly visitor from the land and presided over his career.

The Gods, however, were not content with the city-state of Larsa. They were preparing unpleasant times, although they did so with the appearance of deceitful gifts. The population of Larsa thrived and grew with abundant harvests. At the capital, the Royal Court flourished, attracting vast hordes of absentee landlords, merchants, artisans and purveyors. The Priests of the Temple, who, as spokesmen of the gods, had shared power with the King, now fought a losing battle with the King's ambition. Slowly, Temple lands fell prey to the Court's needs. Money and produce poured into the capital to support the Court and the army. Very little returned to the country for repair of the irrigation system which supported them all.

Lu-igisa dated the change in Larsa's fortunes with the appearance of Thorn-wood in his district. In those early days the man had been little better than an overseer, and a brutal one at that, hiring out for odd jobs. He guaranteed a work force of no more than a dozen men. Lu-igisa had used him only once, and had been so disgusted by Thorn-wood's treatment of the casual labor in his employ, that he had dismissed the man with a reprimand before the end of the job, paying him full wages. Thorn-wood, however, had not drifted away.

Each year the demands of the capital became more pressing. The local administrations were expected not only to raise their own repair budgets, but to supply funds to the Royal Treasury through bribes to help the King in his battle against the Temple. Laws were passed encouraging private contractors to undertake canal work. To protect their wealth against increasingly uneven harvests and the royal appetite, the large landholders of Lu-igisa's district formed a syndicate. Secretly this syndicate made an agreement with Thorn-wood guaranteeing him contracts in return for low bids. The system worked at the expense of the small landholders, whom Thorn-wood overcharged exorbitantly. When the small landholders could not pay, Thorn-wood made use of the brutal distraint law, seizing the women and servants of the debtor household and so manipulating the contract that eventually the debtor and his lands became Thorn-wood's. In addition to these debt-slaves, Thorn-wood employed casual immigrant labor whom he short-changed and sent out of the country when they complained. With his illegal profits, Thorn-wood was able to pay kickbacks to the large landholders and to pour money into the Royal Treasury in the form of bribes.

Although Lu-igisa was guaranteed the Great Canal by his official position, he had to bid against Thorn-wood on other large jobs. His bids were almost always undercut. When Nur-Sin upbraided him, he tried to explain his position. In his naïveté, he thought his chief did not know what was happening in the field. Lu-igisa made it a policy to carry debtor landholders over the lean years, refusing to use the evil weapon of distraint, not only because of the loss of his first wife and child under that system, but because he felt the small landholder was the bulwark of the old values. He frowned upon the use of migratory labor and scorned bribery and kickbacks.

Nur-Sin had been discreetly sympathetic. After all, they had worked together for many years. But he too had pressures on him, and he warned Lu-igisa that he had better find a way to accommodate the needs of the capital. Lu-igisa tried. He cut his costs as best he could. He

[38]

reduced the wages of his entire district administration, especially his own. He brought pressure on his debtor landholders. Secretly he contributed large portions of his own private grain to the general fund, in effect, paying for work done for other landholders. Gradually he went into debt. Nur-Sin was grateful, and Lu-igisa's credit rose at Court—for a while. Then came the Nippur-Isin War.

Unquestionably the seizure of the feeder canal off the Euphrates north of Isin was a brilliant tactical victory, and the construction of the reservoir and fort there had been strategically astute. However, Nippur and Isin would not soon forget this robbery of their water; they were dangerous enemies for an uncertain future. Worst of all, in Lu-igisa's opinion, more water would only hasten the death of the land. The King's demands had exhausted the earth, which already had been over-irrigated to sustain the burgeoning population of the palace city. Lu-igisa had spoken openly against the war in the capital, even before his sons died. From that time on, Nur-Sin's heart had hardened towards him.

Lu-igisa's journeys to the capital were no longer joyous. The urban gentry held the countryside in contempt. It was impossible for Lu-igisa to communicate with people whose soft hands, which barely touched fingers at greeting, had never known the feel of true fertile soil, or the horrible texture of thick clods of clay. The city gentry had never seen a silted furrow. Even Arnabtum, his mistress, was unsympathetic to his warnings. Life at court had become very difficult for her, particularly as she aged, and Lu-igisa's sermonizing exasperated her. She countered with wisdom of her own: "We must bend like reeds to the new winds, or we will break." When they walked in the streets, their hands no longer clasped.

At last the inevitable occurred. Nur-Sin awarded the main Northwest Canal to Thorn-wood. Distraught, Lu-igisa wrote a letter to his mistress at the capital. Immediately after dispatching the letter, Lu-igisa bundled up his family and sent them with a band of friendly nomads over the border to await his bidding at the house of a distant cousin, a citizen of Ur. His letter was returned with Arnabtum's reply a few days later.

The next day Lu-igisa gave his servants and farmworkers a holiday, sending them to the local market fair. For hours he wandered over his entire land, now and then stopping to pick up a handful of soil, letting it run through his fingers. Later he stood for a long time on the bank of the canal, staring down at the waters rushing from the mountains to the sea. In the afternoon, he returned home and fell into an exhausted sleep. Late in the night, he awoke and stepped out onto his sleeping roof, where he began to pace, muttering to himself. A warm breeze blew from the east. High in the sky, the moon, a small brilliant disk, shone down, illuminating the great flat plain cut into regular plots surrounded by embankments. Far to the west he could see the dikes of the great river along which the road to the capital ran. Here and there among the fields, orchards of shade trees spread out their new leaves, which would protect the tender crops from the scorching summer sun. The fields had already been deliberately flooded, and the receding waters had left the muddy soil ready for ploughing and seeding. Wheat and barley would soon rise between the date palms, the olive groves, and the plantations of figs and vines.

Lu-igisa sighed. All this fertility had been his responsibility for so many years. He shuddered as if a chill wind had suddenly sprung up out of that land. That precious dark soil, out of which his people had taken their life, had aged as the hairs of his own head. Under the spring moon, it seemed as if the very soil had silvered from the choking salts that had accumulated over the many years of man's stewardship. Where once the yield had been measured in thousands of liters, now it was measured in hundreds. Everywhere barley was planted instead of wheat; everywhere the demands upon fertile earth were becoming more and more intense to support the great bureaucracy, the intrigue, and the luxury of those who were trying to destroy him, loyal servant of the state, guardian of the soil, tamer of the waters.

"Why?" he cried out, waving his fist. "Oh why have you taken my canal away from me and given it to another?"

And the moon shone down implacably, glinting off the moist soil so that the land turned white. The unhappy official turned abruptly and ran into his house. In a moment, he returned with an incense burner, a small jug of sacramental wine, and the short-handled hoe of his great-granduncle. He knelt, lit the incense, poured out the wine into a goblet and raised his right hand towards the moon:

O Sin, O Nannar, glorified one,
Sin, unique one, who makes bright,
Who furnishes light for people
To guide the dark-headed people aright:
Bright is thy light in heaven,
Bright is thy torch like fire,
Thy brightness has filled the broad land.

I have spread out for thee a pure incense-offering of the night;
 I have poured out for thee the best sweet drink.
I am kneeling; I tarry thus; I seek after thee
On account of the evil of bad and unfavorable portents and signs
 which have happened in my palace and my country.
Bring upon me wishes for well-being and justice.
May my god and my goddess, who for many days have been
 angry with me,
In truth and justice be favorable to me; may my road be
 propitious; may my path be straight.

Even in prayer his voice faltered, his memory failed. Slowly, his hand dropped and he sat back on his haunches. A slight warm breeze passed over the roof. He sniffed, hoping for the deep fresh aroma of earth and new leaves. Instead, an acrid metallic odor wrinkled his nose; he was sure he could smell the salts rising to destroy his people.

Lu-igisa picked up the short-handled hoe of his great-granduncle and stood, letting his hand run over the smooth wood. In Sumeria they had invented much more sophisticated implements since—they even had a plough these days which not only turned the ground behind strong oxen, but seeded the furrows simultaneously through a funnel attached to the frame. Still, this ancient tool remained the favorite of all his people. This hoe had dug canals, built dams, prepared soil for sowing, raised mud-walled houses for people, stalls for cattle and sheep; it had constructed the glorious streets of the capital, the palace, and the city walls, and had helped raise the great monumental ziggurat upon which the Temple stood. Lu-igisa, "Kind-faced Man," held out his hoe to the moon and prayed that time would reverse itself, that the land would be saved from its inevitable destruction by the Thorn-woods, the Nur-Sins, and the Sumuels of this world.

Slowly Lu-igisa's arm dropped. He knew it would only be a matter of time before Larsa fell before the power of neighboring cities or the wandering nomads who watched from over the mountains. But the fall of the city was a small thing compared to the fate which this good man knew lay waiting for all mankind in the future. An end to all order lay ahead.

During the Nippur-Isin War, a month after he had buried his two eldest sons, he had been granted a vision which had visited him regularly thereafter, sometimes in his sleep, and sometimes at an unguarded waking moment. It was a vision of whiteness which caused him to tremble fearfully for hours afterwards. That whiteness was not empty, peaceful and soothing as it should have been, but violent in its purity and punishing in its brilliance. Tonight, gazing at the wet fields reflecting the hard moonlight, he felt that he had entered his terrifying dream forever.

Lu-igisa descended to his office on the ground floor. Carefully he removed all of his records and carried them up to the sleeping porch where he stacked them. It took him much of the night to clear out his office. Then he walked out onto his fields, carrying the short-handled hoe. Wherever he came to a sluice gate, he hammered at it until it fell into splinters; wherever he found a dam, he dug it out. Again and again he chanted the fearful ancient lines aloud:

> Its canal boat towpaths grew nothing but weeds,
> Its chariot roads grew nothing but the 'wailing plant,'
> Moreover, on its canal boat towpaths and landings,
> No human being walks because of the wild goats, vermin, snakes,
>   and mountain scorpions,
> The plains where grew the heart-soothing plants, grew nothing but
>   'reeds of tears'.

Chanting and sweating furiously, Lu-igisa, the "Kind-faced Man," did violence to his own creation.

> O let the tired land blow away and rest in the skies,
> Let it seek its rest down in the salt sea.
> Come egret, duck, carp and eel,
> Return to your springtime marsh,
> Come roaring long-maned lion;

Ram with spreading horn,
Panther, jackal, hyena,
Humped bison and wild boar.
All reclaim your earth from the black-headed people.
Come Air, Come Fire, Come Water, Come Earth—
Create a new and empty world.

Lu-igisa arrived at the great sluice gate of the Etellum Canal. He gazed down on the rushing spring flood waters which had only recently declined slightly from their high mark. Fondly his eye traveled up and down the long lines of his own canal. Then he began to swing and hack and labor mightily. But the task was not easily accomplished. Just as the first light of day broke, he created a small breach through which a flume of water gushed, disintegrating the broken upper board. It was as if the Gods understood his endeavor and lent him the force of the waters. Now he clambered down on the field side until his legs were deep in the cold water, hacking and wedging with his hoe, until he managed to loosen the second and third boards. Showered now with a deluge of water, he deliberately attacked the lower boards. Suddenly, the entire structure gave way, loosing a torrent of water and silt which pinned Lu-igisa's body to the gate sill and buried him. Water filled the feeder ditch within seconds, rushing through all the breaches which Lu-igisa had created, flooding his land.

Several years later, during the great drought, a skeleton was discovered at the great sluice gate, wedged at the very bottom of the early excavation, a skeleton with a firm grasp on an ancient short-handled hoe.

Epilogue

This is a tale which begins in whiteness and ends in whiteness. It is the story of the ingenious method the Gods devised to fill the land and prepare it for the people; it is the story of how the people did not understand what to do with their gifts, and how the Gods punished them.

In the beginning there was nothing but the great salt sea and the mountains. The stormy south wind began to blow, sucking up moisture

[43]

from the sea into billowing white clouds which swept northwards and deposited their whiteness in the form of snowflakes upon the peaks. As spring approached, the snow melted, rushing down stream beds, rivulets and creeks, white snow melting into white water, rushing along, carrying rocks and earth down the sides of the mountains, carving out channels and joining into streams. Finally all the water came together in two rivers which descended the same side of the world, dumping their precious cargo of earth at the base of the mountains. Slowly, as the years passed, the deposited earth pushed the sea off the flanks of the mountains and formed a plain cut by two stately rivers.

Now this plain was a very changeable creature. Every spring the rivers flooded her until she resembled her own mother sea, and then receded leaving a muddy morass, ripe for the life-giving sun. Soon, on the backslopes of the riverbanks a great flowering took place; petals of every shape and color bent to the light breezes. From the water itself, vast marshes of reeds and water lilies bloomed. All manner of egret, duck and waterfowl came to feed in the rich mud. Humped bison strolled along the banks, as did lions and wild boar. Carp and eel spawned in the rich muddy shallows. But the sun was not content. Every day it baked this wondrous vegetation, turning green to brown, withering life away. Winds from the northwest lifted the powdery choking earth-flesh off the surface into the sky, carrying it out over the oceans, as if to return everything to its beginning. Then winter returned with the moist south wind and its clouds, sweeping northwards towards the mountains, and the cycle went on.

Now Enlil, God of the Winds, was not at all satisfied. He found it wasteful that the beautiful flowering plain should bake to nothingness every year, that it should be overwhelmed with great floods, and that animals should wax and wane with the seasons. And Enki, God of Waters Eternal, was extremely dissatisfied that he should have given up so much space to the great plain, only to see it turned into a dry desert year after year. And Ninhursag, the great Mother Earth, out of whose passion all living things were born, was wroth to see her children die yearly, and to see her flesh raised up in clouds of dust on Enlil's breath. So the three gods came together and decided that this wild system which created and destroyed without order should be tamed. This is why, out

[44]

of the fertile mud of the spring plains, they made the black-headed people. Into each new human they pumped a small portion of seawater, and into their lungs they breathed the air of heavens. And when the black-headed people stood, new and amazed at the base of the great mountains, the three gods gave them the great plains in return for a promise: that they would keep the earth fertile and insure that life continue in an orderly fashion all the year long.

The black-headed people looked around them. They saw the fertile levees left by spring floods; they saw the water standing in pools at the slope bottoms. They devised ways to keep the water in the pools long after the floods had vanished, drawing the water out to moisten the rich earth, even under the harsh summer sun. They did this by working together, each one helping the other. Villages grew up, dedicated to the promise they had made to the Gods. But as the land flowered, and the people grew in numbers, the task of providing water to the earth became increasingly difficult. Villages joined other villages, and soon cities were formed with many leaders, all striving to tame the waters. The people began to bank the rivers, to dig canals, and alter the shapes of the rivers to suit their convenience. They created their own canals and ditches to bring water to fields far from the rivers. Each new task required new specialists, and the coordination of all the specialists, along with the farmers and herdsmen, required superintendents and foremen and clerks. To maintain this new order and organization, the black-headed people invented writing on tablets, wedge-shaped marks, tracks of the great world order. Soon the black-headed people became so busy that they forgot the Gods.

To remind them of their debt, the Gods sent silt to clog the canals. Every day the black-headed people had "to do earths," removing the silt, freeing the water, and as they did so, they remembered the Gods. They appointed priests to help give thanks; they built great mounds on top of which they erected temples; and throughout the year they gave elaborate festivals with sacrifices to placate the Gods. Patiently the black-headed people worked and worshipped. They grew in numbers. Their cities and temples and earthworks spread over the plain. But something had gone wrong. The black-headed people had become greedy. In spite of the silt, they began to take the land for granted. Fewer and fewer of

[45]

them actually touched the earth itself. Great hierarchies grew up in the Temple, in the Palace, and in the Marketplace, vying with one another for power.

As the years passed, the Palace and the Marketplace formed an alliance to rob the Temple. Soon the King and the City itself began to replace the Eternal Gods as objects of worship. Now the Gods became very angry. To scourge the people, they sent winds and rainstorms. Increasingly, the earth refused to bear. Worst of all, the Gods decreed that salt should come in from the sea, and down from the mountains, contaminating the groundwater and turning earth itself to clay, choking the roots of all the crops. In desperation the cities turned outwards, hoping to repair their fortunes through conquest. Neighbor fought neighbor, until all their resources had been exhausted. Soon the white salted earth was a desolate barren desert with nothing but bleaching bones and buried treasures, and a few eroding mounds to mark the passing of the black-headed people. This is the end of Lu-igisa's tale.

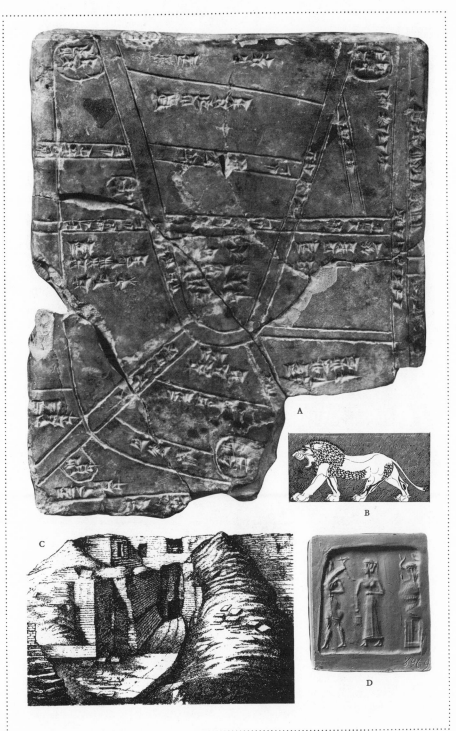

A

B

C

D

E

F

G

L

M

N

O

A Map of fields belonging to the palace and to the priests, Nippur, Sumer, reproduced by permission of the University Museum, University of Pennsylvania.

B Enameled lion from the great door of the palace, Nineveh, Assyria.

C Excavations at Ur, Sumer.

D Cylinder seal impressions, Nippur, Sumer, reproduced by permission of the University Museum, University of Pennsylvania.

E Irrigation, Afej, Iraq, modern times, reproduced by permission of the University Museum, University of Pennsylvania.

F King of Larsa bearing a basket of earth, courtesy Museum of Fine Arts, Boston, Otis Norcross Fund.

G "Shadulf," an irrigation machine of the Nile River, similar to those used in ancient Babylonia.

H Libation scene on a shell plaque, Ur, Sumer, reproduced by permission of the University Museum, University of Pennsylvania.

I Worshipper, Sumer, about 3000 B.C., courtesy of The Metropolitan Museum of Art, Fletcher Fund, 1940.

J Bust, Isin-Larsa, Sumer, between 1900 and 1700 B.C., courtesy Museum of Fine Arts, Boston, Edward J. and Mary S. Holmes Fund.

K Scenes of peace, mosaic-standard, Ur, Sumer, reproduced by permission of the University Museum, University of Pennsylvania.

L Farmer's Almanac, tablet, Nippur, Sumer, reproduced by permission of the University Museum, University of Pennsylvania.

M Head of Gudea, ruler of Lagash, Sumer, about 2200 B.C., courtesy of The Metropolitan Museum of Art, Fletcher Fund, 1949.

N Bronze sickle from Nuzi, Mesopotamia, courtesy of the Peabody Museum, Harvard University.

O Ancient Assyrian method of irrigation.

P Libation ewer, Ur, Sumer, reproduced by permission of the University Museum, University of Pennsylvania.

P

IV

Crossing Over

HULDAH, who helped fashion the great hoop of righteousness to bind her people together under the God of the Word, was born in the palace of the descendants of David, the kings of Judah. Her grandfather, Keeper of the King's Wardrobe, had been a favorite of the wise King Hezekiah, and of his son Manasseh who restored the idols of the Canaanites to the House of the Lord. Huldah, a beautiful, precocious child, was allowed to play with the king's children and to share their meals and the ceremonies of the household. At a very early age she had come to love Baal, God of Clouds and Tempests, and his son Aleyin, "He who rode the shoulders of the clouds, Baal of earth, spirit of rivers and streams and of all things which grew out of the rain's bounty." Huldah wept at the death of Aleyin each year in the dry season, and rejoiced at his rebirth in the autumn.

Huldah's grandfather watched in anguish as she and her cousin Shaphan bowed with the royal children before the idols of the Canaanites. Those were days of darkness and confusion in Judah, which stood between the mighty forces of Assyria and Egypt. The terrible destruction of Judah's sister kingdom, Israel, remained fresh in the memory of the Keeper of the Wardrobe. In his opinion, entrenched corruption and self-indulgence had all but destroyed Judah's spirit and the glory which had been wise King Hezekiah's. Bitterly he inveighed against the cult of the nature gods which flourished in the very palace. To his grandchildren, however, he never showed his anger. Instead, he opened up the royal wardrobe to them as a refuge, and he entertained them with tales of the Nameless One, the invisible God of rainstorm and lightning, of volcano

[53]

and earthquake, whose wrath destroyed the enemies of their people. With glowing eyes, the old man spoke of the Ivriim, "those who crossed over," and of the covenant by which the Lord gave them the fertile land of the Israelite confederacy through which the Lord's water flowed from the snow-capped heights of Lebanon to the sea.

In his wisdom, the old man attempted to teach Huldah and Shaphan the true spirit of the Lord. Often they did not understand his words, but his feeling warmed them and his passionate wooing of their souls flattered them. He told them of Abraham, Moses, and Joshua, and made it seem as if the two children themselves had followed those great leaders across the Euphrates, the Red Sea and the River Jordan. "Waters we have crossed over," he said, taking their young hands into his, gnarled and toughened by the needles of his trade, "and the sacred boundaries of worship. The covenant which Abraham made with the Lord and which Moses renewed brought us this beautiful land in return for our promise to worship Him only, and to abide by his justice." When the old man spoke the word "justice" his large able hands clenched tightly around theirs. "When we crossed over the river to conquer the promised land, we left behind the garden of magic, of charms and potions, we gave up the cruel chaos of nature for a belief in the just community of our people. Only if we continue to act towards one another according to the law and the principles of His justice will the fruits of this land be ours. If we abide by that covenant, never again need we bow down to dim spirits in dark groves, or to fear a multitude of demons rising from the bones of dead animals."

Sitting in the wardrobe, silks and damasks and purple cloths from the south draped around her, Huldah was filled with the love of the God of the covenant. But as soon as she rejoined her playmates in the royal chambers, she once again became the adoring mistress of Baal and Aleyin. Shrewdly she played the game of her elders, threading her way through the intrigues of a land with many gods and with One God.

Huldah reached the age of ten in a year of drought and uncertainty. The kingdom of Judah hesitated between the threats of Egypt and Assyria. The partisans of each power struggled throughout the land. At wit's end, King Manasseh and his mother, who ruled him, consulted the priests, not only those of the One God, but those who served the gods of the earth. Without hesitation, the assembled priests declared that Mot, god of harvest and dry lands where the hot sun always shines, would not release the watery Aleyin until Mot was placated by ancient rites of fire. Every child of the land would have to step through hoops of burning fire, chanting praises to the sun and begging Mot to release his hold on the land. If Mot persisted, then the first-born males of all the families of Judah would be sacrificed to Mot and to the One God.

The party of the devout, among them Huldah's grandfather and her father, protested this barbarous suggestion. There had been such sacrifices in the past, and they had only brought down upon their heads the disastrous wrath of the Lord. In their eyes, human sacrifice was sacrilege. For days Manasseh hesitated. He loved his first-born son Joachim dearly, and he might never have yielded to the priests had it not been for his weak dependence upon his imperious mother, who would gladly have stepped into the flames herself if her priests had so decreed.

The command went out. People gathered upon all the sacred heights of the land. Solemnly, the royal family climbed the steps to the Second Mount next to the Great Pool. This reservoir for the city was dry now, its bottom cracked like a shattered vessel. Pyres of faggots studded a central ring in the Great Pool itself. Out of each pyre rose numerous stakes. To the north, rams, bulls, goats, and heifers, first-born beasts groomed for sacrifice, milled about in pens, bleating and lowing and snorting. But their sound was as a whisper to the wails of the people as they led their own dear sons to slaughter.

First, amidst groaning chants, all the children were made to step through hoops of fire. As the fearful flames shot up her calves and thighs, Huldah prayed for rain to Aleyin, to Baal and to Yahweh, the One God. The sun beat down mercilessly upon their heads.

Huldah watched the king's eldest son, the good and kind Joachim, bound to the highest stake in the midst of the dried and cracking pool. Beside him were bound her own brother, her eldest cousin, and all the other first-born sons of the palace. Huldah never turned her gaze from the face of Joachim as the flames shot up around him. Hours later, at the very feet of those charred mournful stakes, the animals were slaughtered in honor of the many gods and the One God, Yahweh, their flesh roasted and eaten in a great feast which lasted two days.

[55]

On the day after the sacrifice and feast, Huldah's grandfather died in a fire which completely gutted the royal wardrobe. Several days later, Huldah's father, a much decorated soldier, was killed in an abortive attempt to depose the king. Within hours, Huldah and her mother were cast out of the palace.

Eventually the rains came, but few believed that Manasseh's terrible sacrifice had in any way been helpful. Even though Judah flourished again, its terraced lands amazingly fertile, the luxury of its cities equalling that of the great kingdoms to the north and south, despair seized the hearts of the people. The cults of Baal and Aleyin and Ashtaroth grew in power and excess, their rites providing the only relief from the fears which lurked in the souls of this people, cursed now with the memory of that abominable sacrifice.

∵

From the age of ten to the age of thirteen, Huldah wandered through the land with her widowed mother, gleaning what she could from back kitchens of the rich and the charity of the devout. When they were caught taking meager leavings from harvested fields, they were whipped and jailed as thieves.

In Judah of that time, the poor followed the poor, camping out under bridges, in caves, or deep in forests, hoping to escape the periodical labor roundups of the king's soldiers. Hordes of farmers, ruined by the drought, wandered about the countryside with their families. Huldah and her mother joined them, hoping to find some comfort in the fellowship of poverty. Among these people, itinerant prophets found sympathetic ears to their cries against the rich and their prophecies of the inexorable doom of Judah. Huldah loved to listen to these strange men, finding in their words a memory of her beloved grandfather. One, in particular, impressed her: a very young man with a narrow long face, skin as brown as a nut and wrinkled as a fig, and eyes the color of deep mountain pools. She thrilled to hear him sing out praises for the water of the Lord and exulted in his angry denunciation of the terrible sacrifice by fire.

"Cut off thine hair, O Jerusalem," he shouted, "and cast it away, and take up a lamentation on the bare heights; for the Lord hath rejected and forsaken the generation of his wrath. For the children of Judah have done that which is evil in my sight, saith the Lord: they have set their abominations in my house which is called by my name, to defile it. And they have built the high places of Tophet, which is in the valley of Hinnom, to burn their sons and their daughters in the fire; which I commanded not, neither came it into my mind."

The consuming flames of the Second Mount haunted Huldah's dreams. She often woke, crying out for water; sweating in fear, her limbs burned. But she did not know which god to blame for the fiery murders of the young men of Judah, and her own scorched limbs. Baal and Aleyin had withheld their waters, but then, so had Yahweh, the One God. In her rage against the evil fortune which had befallen her and her mother, Huldah was tempted to forsake all the gods. Later, watching the sumptuous processions of the plump worshippers of Baal, her childish wonder at the billowing clouds and sinuous rivers and all the green growing plants returned.

In confusion and suffering, Huldah approached womanhood. Men began to notice her; their eyes lingered on her body, their hands reached out to grasp at her. Fearing for her daughter, Huldah's mother sought out sanctuary in the temples devoted to the One God. She hoped to arrange a marriage with one of the devout before she passed away. Unfortunately, by that time, almost all the temples had opened their gates to accommodate all of the gods of the land.

One day, Huldah's mother chose the wrong temple for refuge. It was a day of festivals to the strange gods. Fearing the drunken processions through the streets, Huldah's mother had fled the city on the coast where they had been begging. She had planned to spend the night on the beach, but stiff winds blew up from the sea, driving dark clouds towards the shore. The only shelter she could find was in the portico of the great coast temple.

As soon as they arrived, she knew she had made a mistake. This temple was the home of the sacred prostitutes of Ashtaroth. Celebrants lounged about the temple steps, drinking and waiting their turn. Ordinary prostitutes set up a brisk business around the temple. Huldah's mother tried to turn back down the road, but a troop of soldiers appeared, pushing a new crowd in front of them. Although the soldiers had orders to clear the temple steps, they chased only the men away; when their officers disappeared inside the temple, they began to use whatever women they found.

Desperately, Huldah and her mother rushed towards the temple entrance, hoping to throw themselves on the mercy of the priests. Before they could gain the top step, they were seized and thrown down. As Huldah was being raped on the steps of the temple high on the cliffs above the sea, she saw the clouds come scudding in, filled with their life-giving waters. In terror she sought the comfort of Yahweh, but his imageless power escaped her. Instead, she saw only Aleyin riding his father's shoulders towards the shore. At the moment she felt her body penetrated, she dedicated herself to Baal's son.

Below, two soldiers fought over her mother, tearing the frail body between them. She heard her mother's death cry; her own powerful voice rose to join her mother's departing spirit; and the skies exploded with fire and thunder, sending down a hailstorm which chased the soldiers to cover. Huldah crawled down the steps towards her mother. Battered by hail, she cradled the lifeless body. A deluge of rain followed, washing their blood down the marbled steps. The priests found her there.

∵

In the temple, where she was put in the care of the sacred prostitutes, Huldah came awake to life with an intensity which amazed all around her. Her hands were constantly in motion, touching everyone and everything—silks, leaves, flesh—like the hands of a blind woman eager to discover the secrets of a dark world. The aroma of a flower, of roasted meat, of perfume excited her equally. But she did not laugh; she seldom spoke, and late in the night, her muffled sobs could be heard for hours.

Six months after her arrival at the temple—at the age of fifteen—Huldah became a sacred prostitute. Her angry, wild beauty flowered at the drunken orgies which accompanied the feasts of dedication to the gods of the earth.

Huldah loved her body passionately; she did not love herself. It was as if her body were simply another gift, like the dark groves of cypress on the bluffs, the spring down in the rocky canyon, or the carpet of anemones on distant hills. When Huldah shared her body for the night, she mined it for every sensation it could offer. And even as she gave herself up to her body, she felt herself wandering through the regions of her past, blessed and cursed by the many gods and the One God. She danced before Mot's consuming flames with violent seductiveness, daring that awesome god to embrace her, for in her loins he would find the burning death he had visited on Aleyin and on those young men, high on the Second Mount above Jerusalem.

At the very height of her pleasure, a strange melodic wail of grief rose up out of her stomach, a song of the stinking quarters of the poor among whom she had almost suffocated as a child, a song of emaciated hands ripping stale bread from her grasp, of the pinched faces of childish mothers suckling babies at withered breasts, and of men with lifeless eyes watching the plump bodies parade by to and from the temple. Even as her loins began to shudder, in her ears rang the voice of that grim young prophet shouting out: "And I will stretch over Jerusalem the line of Samaria, and the plummet of the house of Ahab; and I will wipe Jerusalem as a man wipeth a dish, wiping it and turning it upside down."

At the age of twenty-five, Huldah was crowned High Priestess, Ashtaroth's living double, in the coastal temple. Only two days later, returning from a walk along the cliffs, she found herself confronted by that same prophet who had thrilled her during her exile. There he stood on the very steps where she and her mother had been assaulted, his face still young, nut-brown and lined with sorrowful knowledge. His hair had turned white. The crowd surrounding him parted as she approached and she found herself caught in the depth of those staring blue-black eyes.

"The temple of the Lord," he called out, "the temple of the Lord, the temple of the Lord are these!"

Down below, the great waves swept in from the sea just as they had on that frightful day; above, the clouds, heavy with water, scudded towards land. The prophet continued.

"And I brought ye into a plentiful land, to eat the fruit thereof and the goodness thereof; but when ye entered, ye defiled my land, and made mine heritage an abomination. The priests said not, Where is the

[59]

Lord? and they that handle the law knew me not: the rulers transgressed against me, and the prophets prophesied by Baal, and walked after things that do not profit."

Huldah drew near the man, grieving for her father and her wise grandfather. She gazed into eyes the color of deep mountain pools and saw no lust there. She listened to the wild voice cry out for the fatherless, the widow, and the stranger, and she grieved for her broken mother, gleaning in the empty fields of the rich.

"Thine own wickedness shall correct thee, and thy backslidings shall reprove thee: know therefore and see that it is an evil thing and a bitter, that thou hast forsaken the Lord thy God and that my fear is not in thee."

The cheeks of the High Priestess Ashtaroth, Mother of Baal, turned crimson, and she hung her head with shame.

"For of old time thou hast broken the yoke, and burst the bands; and thou saidst, I will not serve; for upon every high hill and under every green tree thou didst bow thyself, playing the harlot."

Huldah fled into the temple. She stood before the ark gazing at the gleaming brown of the waxed acacia bound with golden clasps which guarded the treasures of the Word of the Lord. Her grandfather had taught her how to read that Word, and how to copy out the shapes of its letters. She remembered the feel of the parchment. She longed for the cool parchment and the bold strokes of the pen by which the law found its expression. Through the open door of the sanctuary rang the prophet's voice: "Shall the snow of Lebanon fail from the rock of the field? Or shall the cold waters that flow down from afar be dried up? For my people hath forgotten me, they have burned incense to vanity.

"He hath made the earth by his power, he hath established the world by his wisdom, and by his understanding hath he stretched out the heavens.

"When he uttereth his voice, there is a tumult of waters in the heavens, and he causeth the vapors to ascend from the ends of the earth; he maketh lightnings for the rain, and bringeth forth the wind out of his treasuries."

Huldah remained before the ark for many hours. That night she returned to her chambers, bathed and put on simple black garments. She came back to the ark, opened it and removed the heavy scroll covered with fine cloth and gold plates. Carefully she laid the scroll upon the altar, removed the cover and by the light of a lamp, began to read those words, running her fingertips over the parchment. As she read of the Lord and His law, her heart was soothed, and she felt herself surrounded by her lost family. In the morning, the priests found her there, still reading. They dared not reproach her, for she had become even more powerful than they.

When Huldah had finished her reading, she replaced the scroll in the ark and left the temple to seek the prophet Jeremiah.

∴

For several years Huldah followed Jeremiah in his wanderings. Wherever they were, through his influence, she was given access to the sacred documents. When she had heard and read enough, she took her leave of the prophet and sought refuge high in the mountain wilderness of Lebanon. There, where the waters of the Lord began their journey to the sea, she lived in a cave, fed by occasional herders. For months she punished herself, seeking to purge her soul of its unclean yearnings, to calm her hungry body, and to find peace in the Lord. One winter day, a blizzard surprised her far from her cave. After struggling for some hours, she fell to the ground, exhausted. She might have died there, had she not heard the voice of her grandfather calling out through the wind, bidding her rise and return to her cave. When she was safe and warm in the cave, and had fallen asleep, the voice of her grandfather continued in her ears:

"Rivers of water we have left behind, but we remain immersed in the waters of time. Today, the community of our people has shattered into fragments. Without justice we cannot continue to live in history; we will be forced to return to nature. If those who crossed over are to survive, justice must be restored."

The voice of Huldah's grandfather ceased, and Huldah slept for three days. She awoke with the memory of his words and the knowledge she must help her people make another crossing.

Not long thereafter, the prophetess Huldah took up lodging in the second quarter of Jerusalem and sent for her cousin Shaphan, scribe in the palace and tutor to the child King Josiah. Of the entire family of the keeper of the wardrobe, only Shaphan had managed to keep his footing on the slippery floors of the palace.

When Shaphan came to his cousin bearing a simple earthenware jar full of the icy waters of mountain springs, Huldah knew that he had not forgotten the days they had sat, arms entwined, at the foot of their grandfather. Huldah took the jar and drank deeply. She handed it to her cousin who sipped a small portion. She could see that he was still afraid, even with the word of the Lord in his heart. She took his hand and comforted him, and then told him of her sojourn high in the mountain wilderness. She reminded him of their grandfather's story of the people who had crossed over. Shaphan understood her words and nodded agreement, even when she added: "But we in Judah have stepped back into the magic garden. We have broken the covenant and lost the law. The Lord will break this nation and scatter it over the earth unless . . ." Until dawn they talked of what they must do to prevent the destruction of their beloved nation.

Huldah continued to live in the second quarter, a poor district jammed with peasant families who had been forced off the land, first by natural disasters—droughts, hailstorms, insect and disease plagues— and then by the unscrupulous speculations of the rich who loaned them money at usurious rates and took their land from them when they could not pay. Mysterious well-born strangers, hidden and cloaked, visited her house late at night. The women gossiped about her, claiming that her visitors received more than prophecies during their visits. They found something suggestive in her walk and a taste for the gaudy in her clothes; they claimed they recognized in her eyes a need so strong, a glint of desire which would make everything male within a hundred paces tremble at her passing. When she spoke in public, however, the women forgot their meanness and stood enthralled, for Huldah had the true gift of prophecy, and a voice, deep and grinding in its timbre.

Against the temple priests who bowed to Baal and to Egypt, Huldah preached the word of Yahweh/Elohim, God of justice, protector of the widow, the orphan, the stranger and the poor. Standing on high places outside the city wall, her arms outspread, her face bared to the heavens, she uttered prophecies of the doom of Judah.

[62]

When she was not prophesying publicly, Huldah seldom left her rooms. Cooked food was brought by the wife of the tavern-keeper who reported, with astonishment, that within the closed room, the prophetess spent the entire day and most of the night reading from ancient parchment scrolls and writing. In Judah, women were never taught to read, and few men could write. Furthermore, said the gossip, Huldah's mysterious guests were not pleasure-seeking nobles, but a roomful of lawyers, clerks, scribes, and priests, each holding up a different scroll, attempting to drown out the others with his arguments.

For eighteen years, while Shaphan nursed the young King Josiah upon the new doctrine and recruited sympathetic members of the government and the priesthood, Huldah occupied herself with a complete revision of the law. Until that time, Hebrew justice had been based upon fragments of the scripture, some with the name Yahweh, others with the name Elohim, each containing contradictory strictures and observances. The confusion of the laws had provided ample excuse for landholders, judges, and priests to grow wealthy at the expense of the nation. The entire reform of Huldah and Shaphan rested upon their ability to create a single true text of the laws. And so, with the help of a devoted minority, Huldah labored to produce this text which would then be delivered to the people of Judah as the word God handed down to Moses.

This revision of the law was to be the cornerstone of Josiah's reform by which he would purge all gods except for Yahweh/Elohim, the One God. Temples, sacred grottos, forest shrines, and high altars were all to be thrown down, leaving only the temple in Jerusalem, controlled by the king. Thus the power of Judah would once more be concentrated in the palace, all worship monitored, and the corrupt influence of the unfaithful priesthood curbed.

When the law of Moses had been finally rewritten, Huldah and her conspirators sent for the finest scribe in Judah to prepare a counterfeit of ancient scrolls. This they set in an old chest of acacia, all bound with brass, and hid it in a recess below a false floor in the temple in Jerusalem.

The events which followed were thus related in later histories: "And in the eighteenth year of Josiah's reign, he sent Shaphan to oversee the repair of the House of the Lord God in Jerusalem. And the workmen there, the carpenters, the builders, the hewers of stone and timber, discovered a fine old chest of acacia all bound with brass in a recess below a false floor. And they brought the chest to Hilkiah, the High Priest, who opened it and discovered within, on an ancient parchment, the Book of the Law of the Lord, given to Moses.

"And then King Josiah commanded that Shaphan read the Book of the Law, and when he heard the admonitions of the Lord, he rent his clothes and wept. Then the King commanded that Shaphan and Hilkiah take the book to Huldah, the prophetess of the second quarter, and inquire of her the Lord's intentions. When they came to Huldah and asked her of the Lord, she replied that unless the people reformed, the Lord would bring evil upon Judah and all of its inhabitants for their ways, but that the king would be spared, for his heart was tender and he had humbled himself before the Lord.

"Then the king gathered together all the elders of Judah in Jerusalem, and all the inhabitants, and he read them the words of the Book of the Law that had been found. And the king made a convenant there, before all the elders and the inhabitants of Jersualem, to walk after the Lord and to keep his commandments, and his statutes, and to perform the words of the Book of the Law that had been found. And he caused all those present to stand to the same covenant of the Lord God of their fathers.

"Now the king and the high priest, and all the priests of the second order and the keepers of the door brought forth all the idols and vessels made for Baal and for Ashtaroth, and for all heathen gods and burned them in the fields of Kidron, and they stamped them to powder at the brook Kidron and cast the powder thereof upon the graves of the common people. And Josiah put down the idolatrous priests, whom the kings of Judah had ordained to burn incense in the high places in the cities of Judah; them also that burned incense unto Baal, to the sun, and to the moon, and to the planets, and to all the host of heaven. And Josiah defiled Tophet, which is in the valley of the children of Hinnom, so that no man might make his son or his daughter to pass through the fire of Molech. And finally King Josiah took away the horses that the kings of Judah had given to the sun, at the entering in of the House of the Lord, and he burned the chariots of the sun with fire."

∵

And late at night, after the king and his purging procession had left the brook Kidron and the lonely graveyard there, planted with the bones of the poor who had failed in the yoke of wealthy Judah, the prophetess Huldah found herself alone, sitting on the bank, watching the dark waters flow past. Now she too had crossed over for the last time. Her body had been dipped in the waters of the One God, and she had been tempered. Was her fire then quenched? Within the hoop of justice the orphan would be cared for, the widow, the beggar and the stranger, and human flesh would never again be roasted for the pleasure of the gods.

But what had they given up for these precious goods?

Huldah rose and stretched out her arms to the moon, to the empty clouds scudding across the sky, to the willow branches, black against the bright sky. In silence she prayed to the One God and to all the departed gods for the day when the law would encompass not only the minds of men and women, but also their bodies and the body of the living earth.

A

B

C

D

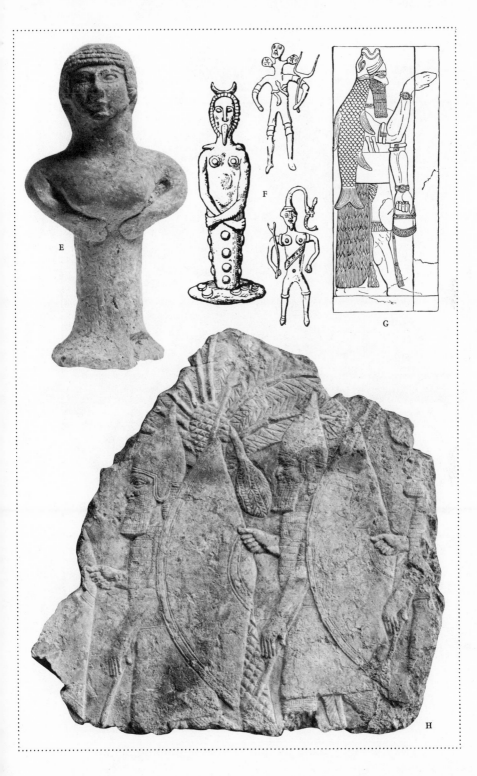

E   F   G   H

I

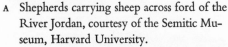

J

K

A Shepherds carrying sheep across ford of the
   River Jordan, courtesy of the Semitic Museum, Harvard University.

B Relief of Marduk-nadin-akhe, king of
   Mesopotamian gods.

C The Fly God.

D Baal, chief god of ancient Canaan.

E Astarte, goddess of love and fertility, a clay
   figurine of Palestine, courtesy of the Lowie
   Museum of Anthropology, University of
   California, Berkeley.

F Three Phoenician idols.

G The God Ea as man-fish from a sculpture at Nimrud.

H Marching soldiers, a relief from the palace of
   Sennacherib at Nineveh, Assyria, 705–681 B.C., courtesy
   Museum of Fine Arts, Boston, Anna M. Richards Fund.

I Mesopotamian god with eagle's head.

J An ancient copy of the Samaritan Pentateuch.

K Standing man from Tell Judeideh, North Syria,
   about 2900 B.C., courtesy Museum of Fine Arts,
   Boston, The Marriner Memorial Syrian Expedition.

V

A Time of Flutes,
A Time of Numbers,
A Time of Things

DUSK. The shadows of the mountains reach out to the plain. Remnants of fallen grain glisten with the light of the skies. An autumn chill seems to rise up out of the earth, penetrating the sun-baked walls of the city. And with the cold comes the almost inaudible sound of a distant flute. A slight shiver goes through the men sauntering through the streets, chatting in conference near the market, making their way homeward from the gymnasium. They pause. Their heads cock. One claps his cold hands together. Another clasps himself roughly about his generous belly. A third gives a shake, like a dog ridding himself of unwelcome water. The moment passes and the men continue homeward. Now, from the heart of the vineyards, all red and yellow as the leaves prepare to drop, the sweet piercing sound stabs at the town. And an answer comes almost immediately from the other side, from among the proud branches of the olive trees vainly guarding themselves from the spoiling hands of men.

In the valley, Theolmus, who has spent the afternoon going over harvest accounts with his foreman, hurriedly concludes his business. With the sound of those harsh flutes in the air, the countryside is safe to no man. He had hoped his ears would never again hear that dreadful sound. He sighs as he mounts his two-wheeled carriage and whips his horse at a fast trot toward the city walls.

Throughout the city the men hurry and then pause, as if they want to get to their houses and yet are unwilling to face what waits for them there. From behind the walls comes an unfamiliar clatter of bells and a clash, like light pieces of armor knocked against one another. The younger men appear to be the most disturbed. A few run through the streets, their brows dark and threatening, only to be pulled up short by the hearty grasp of an older friend who determinedly detains them in conversation: men of experience know that there is nothing to be done once the first flute sounds.

As the light fades from the sky and the shadows of the mountains crawl over the whole land and then over the sea beyond, the odd invading sound of the flutes gathers strength and breaks into a brief melodic line—rude and strong and rhythmic. It is a song from the wild north which stops almost too soon, leaving a frightening silence. And now the bells take up the rhythm left in the evening air by the flutes. Tentatively, metal strikes metal in a clash of cymbals, jarring the fragile composure of the men and sending them rushing through the streets again, eager to be within their own walls before the darkness.

Klytemna, wife of Theolmus, stands unmoving in the midst of the kitchen, where her two maidservants and her daughter are hurriedly finishing preparations for the men's dinner. There are always four or five guests, and more on feast days. Normally, Klytemna would command the preparations, tasting, seasoning, ordering her servants about with great decision, but today, since that first faint sound of the flute, she has stood transfixed in the midst of the kitchen, staring out into the court at the shrine of Zeus, where the family say their daily prayers.

They came from the north and the east, warriors on light two-wheeled chariots, drawn by wondrous ass-like creatures with gentle faces, and flowing neck-hair and tails. 'The People of the Horse,' they called themselves, for that is what they named those creatures: horse. Once, long ago, they had been farmers, settled on distant plains, vast and flat beyond our imagining, for we lived in a mountainous land, with our vines and our goats. They were warriors who preferred to talk and trade, but their weapons were wondrous to behold—light and intricate, made cunningly out of a combination of metals. They owned herds too, cattle, sheep and goats, and they moved like a great army, with discipline and organization, sending out scouts, advance parties. Their merchants prepared the way peacefully wherever possible, mapping out new lands into which their main body would travel. Each troop had its own chief, each worshipped its own particular gods, but all carried this one great sky God named Zeus, God of thunder, and lightning, the God of storms and of the sun. He was no beautiful youngster, this Zeus; he was full in years and commanding; he ruled; and the others, gods and men, obeyed. He was very much like the best of their chiefs.

From somewhere in the next alley, the rhythmic sounds of the cymbals begin; the two maidservants, both from the north, stand upright. They gaze at their mistress, who has scarcely moved since she entered the kitchen, and suddenly they bolt out the door, through the courtyard, disappearing into the street. Klytemna's young daughter cries out and shakes her mother's shoulder. Without a word, Klytemna takes the girl's wrist and leads her to the womens' apartments, where she packs a small bag of the girl's belongings.

"You are a woman now," she says.

Mother and daughter, their shawls wrapped around them, slip out into the streets and make their way through the shadows towards the city gates. At each step they are joined by other women and girls, all hurrying in the same direction. No one greets one another; no one nods; all stare intently towards the mountains. Everywhere now the sound of bells resounds and the girl notices that her mother wears two anklets of bells. Once out of the gate, the women throw open their shawls, calling out strange sounds in answer to the flutes, which play insistently now from the vineyards, from the orchards, and from the mountains. Beyond the fields on the high cliffs, a flame leaps up, and a shout from the women rises to greet the first fire of their own festival—the true festival of the quickened womb and the dying handsome young god whose seed has been spent and buried deep in the earth.

Theolmus enters his house. The dining table is almost completely set for the evening banquet. As he moves about finishing the salad, turning the meats, lowering the fire, and completing the table setting, he wonders whether his guests will appear. The strange silence of the city seizes him like an ache. A cool breeze off the mountains to the north carries faint phrases from the distant flutes and cymbals. Images of frenzied bodies invade his consciousness.

"Wife!" he calls out sternly, then more plaintively, "Daughter!" He paces about the courtyard, raising his arms to the sky. He yearns for

[73]

his sons. The same great force which has drawn his wife and daughter to the hills, drove his sons from his hearth.

"Hippias." The name of his eldest son seldom crosses his lips. The boy has grown to a cold and distant maturity. He has settled in the east, where he spends his days amassing coins, a perfect antidote to the madness of the daemonic spirits which reside deep in his mother's womb.

"Protolcus." The voice of the father softens. His youngest son is his favorite, a boy of deep feeling and clear thought. Protolcus might have been here tonight to sustain him in his lonely vigil had it not been for the bloody tragedy of four years ago. Anguish grinds Theolmus' jaws when he remembers that autumn night, much like this very night, when the flutes had sounded, the mountain fires burned, and that unfortunate troop of young soldiers had made the error of choosing a woody mountain glen for their bivouac. Their intrusion into the mysterious rites had been cruelly punished. Protolcus, one of the few survivors of that bloody night, had been sent into exile for the transgression.

Theolmus drops his arms in defeat. He turns towards the altar of Zeus. An ironic laugh wells up in his throat.

He had been the God of weather, God of the tempest whose lightning and thunder struck down their enemies in the lands through which they travelled. And when they settled down to become farmers again, vintners and cultivators of the olive tree, they immediately arranged a marriage of convenience between their Zeus and the Great Earth Mother, goddess of the native peoples of this place. The 'Horse People' were clever politicians. The marriage greatly diminished the power and the glory of the Great Earth Mother. Zeus was quite a tyrant; he had defeated his own father, who had defeated his father before him. Mother Earth was nothing unless Zeus's rain impregnated her, and so Zeus's power reigned over the lands in which his people had settled. However, Zeus was as restless as his subjects, and soon he went about impregnating all manner of women. They bore a host of rival gods and heroes who wasted their time in devious battles with one another and abortive rebellions against Zeus. The whole business of water and earth soon got lost in matters of adultery, rape, jealous rivalries over wealth and power and political machinations.

One by one the guests of Theolmus slip furtively through the door. None could bear his own empty house or the distant sounds from the hills. Although the banquets are ordinarily occasions for great wit and raillery, each man vying with the other to turn a sharp and pointed

[74]

phrase, each laboring to defeat his companions in exquisite argument, tonight the men are kind and supportive of one another.

Theolmus' guests all served with him on the Commission chosen to deal with those unfortunate events of four years ago—the events which led to the expulsion of Protolcus from the city. The Commission had originated the master plan by which the decaying celebration of Eleusis had been revived in order to still those very flutes which tonight shatter their domestic peace. Until today, they had been optimistic. Realizing that it would be impossible to annihilate the dancing god of the vine who flayed the flanks of their women and sent them howling over the shadowy mountains, these substantial gentlemen had decided to put a ring through the nose of Dionysus and lead him in an orderly fashion into the center of their city in a state procession. They had hoped to absorb not only that rebellious god, but his wild revels and bloody rite into a reasonable public holiday, a city festival.

The Eleusinian Mystery Revised included something for everyone. It was a great show, a marvelous story, good dancing, good acting, good music, good preaching, good food and drink, and even the blood of a thousand pigs to satisfy the deepest forbidden desires. One might have thought the women would have been satisfied. They had included three long processions—forth and back and forth once more to Eleusis—over the rocky hills which separated the great wheat plains of Eleusis from the vine-covered valley of the city. They had even added an initiation which would ensure a happy immortality for anyone who had the money to buy a pig.

For three years now the flutes had been silent. Every year the revived harvest festival of Eleusis had increased in popularity. Again and again citizens had approached to thank the Commission for the great comfort their souls had received from the new and improved Eleusinian Mystery. How the citizens cherished the secret revelation in the great hall, where obscenity and reverence mixed under the awesome symbol of the ripe stalk. "Rain!" they cried, gazing up into the heavens. "Conceive!" they commanded, looking down on earth. It was a rare treasure for the state to deliver freely to its citizens: plenty on earth, and a happy life after death. And yet the Commission had failed in its prime objective. The gift of Eleusis had not satisfied the women.

[75]

The women saw through the charade, and so remained unsatisfied, waiting for the sweet piercing note of the flute; waiting for the discordant jangle of the cymbals, the taste of blood and raw flesh to confirm their total immersion in life.

When his guests depart, Theolmus sits and begins a letter to his youngest son, Protolcus, living in a Chapter House of the Pythagoreans in Italy:

"Dear Son," he writes, "I want to explain myself to you above all, perhaps to find some forgiveness for this failure of mine—of all the fathers. Zeus hides somewhere in the sky, while we cower behind the walls of our cities. And the sacred groves, the rocks, the streams are all left to the wild invasions of that foreign daemon who snatches up our women and dashes them down, estranged in their very wombs from the reasonable rule of their husbands.

"I know it is cruel of me to speak of these matters to you who had to face the horror yourself, but I am alone here now and have no one. Despite our ingenious inventions, our clever politics and flourishing trade, Earth has a way of reasserting herself. The Mother may bow year after year in mock obedience, but she never truly submits to the Father's rule. Poor Zeus does not know when it will happen, but the call comes regularly now from the Great Mother to her sisters and her daughters in a way which cannot be denied.

"I merely want you, son, to know that at last I am beginning to understand your yearning to escape the 'wheel of time.' Until we grow wombs we shall remain separate from the force which gave us birth and sustains us. Your loving father."

∵

Protolcus, younger son of Theolmus, sits panting in a slight declivity, high on a bare hillside in Calabria, Italy. He can see Crotona in the distance, the city walls shimmering in the heat. Just below, in the outskirts of a suburban quarter, a building burns. Black smoke billows up into the empty white sky. Now and then orange-red flames flare out against the dusty green of the trees. He can only imagine the angry sweating crowd which surrounds the building, the men and women chanting, feeding the flames with stray pieces of wood, and laughing at the vain cries for help which come from the victims inside. Protolcus had tried to convince his fellows to flee with him over the wall of the garden plot, but stubbornly they had insisted that they could reason with the mob. And besides, they valued their precious books too much. They will perish now, with the Chapter House of Pythagoras and all their political power will vanish with the smoke. They had valued the things of this world too much and had not lived according to their own teachings.

Blood and dirt stain the young man's white robe. He has cut his forehead badly, scrambling up through the thick brambles of the hillside. He had climbed using only one hand, for in the other he held his lyre, the only possession he considered important enough to save. If he wanted to survive, he would have to get rid of both the white robe and the lyre before morning. The mob would be hunting out the Brotherhood for days to come. Of course, he might choose martyrdom, but only on his own terms. He refused to die protecting earthly power, for which the Brotherhood was justly being punished. Hoping to reform society, they had formed an alliance with the aristocrats and had been brought down with them.

Gently Protolcus' fingers seek the strings of his lyre, sounding out an octave, and then a fifth, and a fourth. He plays no tunes, simply intervals as his mind seeks a resting place in the harmony of the eternal One.

"I am the son of Earth and Heaven," he chants, attempting to revive his spirits. "I am perishing with thirst. Give me to drink of the waters of memory. I come from the pure. I have paid the penalty of unrighteousness. I have flown out of the sorrowful circle of life. Robed in white, I have avoided the taint of childbirth and funerals. I have eaten no meat, nor beans, nor any food scorched with fire. In what have I failed then? Look upon my good works. What have I not done that I ought to have done?"

Certain of his coming death, the young man strokes the strings of his lyre, seeking the Divine Interval, seeking to prepare his soul for its flight. Ambitious even at this extremity, he concentrates all his powers inward to see if his is one of those exceptional souls that leaps out of the horrifying wheel of birth into an eternal union with the rational unchanging Truth. With the name of his blessed leader, Pythagoras of the Golden Thigh, he seeks to blot out the memory of that grimacing mob tearing at the gates, the terrified eyes of his brothers who carried manuscripts here and there in vain attempts to find a safe hiding place. Now to his nostrils the wind carries the smell of burning wood which feeds his animal terror. His heart begins to pound once again. Earthward he falls.

Protolcus looks down on his blood-stained robe. He has never succeeded in a perfect moment of contemplation. No matter how hard he tries to fix his mind on the rational unchanging truth of existence, the very form, proportion and pattern of all things based upon the ultimate fact of Number, his earthly memories intervene. Every time he feels he is on the very sill of eternity, his mind already thrilling at the light and warmth radiating out of the unity of the Single Monad, a tickle of fear touches him somewhere in the middle of his stomach, and the terrible darkness of that autumn night of chaos long ago in the mountains near his home city takes possession of his body and soul, plunging him headlong back into earthly sin. Instead of the Master's smiling face in the sunny garden, out of the dark looms his mother, crowned with the horns of a ram, cloaked with the skin of a bull, eyes glazed, teeth and lips dripping with blood.

The young soldiers had chosen a remote mountain glen for their last bivouac on the autumn maneuvers. They camped on a ledge just above the canyon floor, well hidden by the brush and a thick grove of pine. At midnight they had been awakened by the sound of flutes and cymbals. To their amazement, a procession of shaggy creatures wearing the skins of beasts, with horns on their heads and enormous penises jutting out before them, came dancing into the clearing below followed by a crowd of bewildered girls hurried along by older women who danced and sang and clapped cymbals together. The young girls formed in a large circle. Each was given a skin of beverage and forced to drink. As the music began in earnest, the girls were led in a round dance which kept increasing in tempo. At first the girls seemed shy and intent upon keeping rhythm, but soon the excitement of the older women proved contagious, and the girls began to dance with passion. At intervals the music ceased, and the drink was passed around.

The soldiers realized that they had stumbled upon the initiation rites of the mountain deity. Below them were the young girls of their city, about to become women. It was a sight forbidden to men. They knew they should have fled, but the ceremony hypnotized them. These were their sisters, their future wives, their mothers and aunts. Fires cast an eerie light upon the glen.

The young soldiers crept down from their ledge towards the ceremony. Heartsick, they gazed with envy at the great bulging penises of the beasts. Then a new sound filled the air: the lowing of bulls, the bellowing of goats, the rumbling of hooves, and the shrill yips and shouts of women. Across the valley floor came a new troop of women chasing several bulls and a small herd of goats. As the women ran, they tore at the animals and whipped them with branches. This new troop burst upon the dancers, who joined the chase about the valley floor.

At this moment the troop of young soldiers was discovered. A silence fell over the women. Only the lowing of the injured beasts could be heard. Women and girls stood rigid, peering at the young men. The lieutenant stood and took a step forward, as if to explain his error. Immediately, thirty women pounced upon him and dragged him to the middle of the clearing. The cymbals sounded, the flutes sang, and the chase was on again. The other soldiers scattered. Along with the animals, they were run to the ground. Protolcus shrank back out of the light, and crawled through the foliage looking for a hollow log or a cave in the cliff wall. Before he could reach safety, one of the shaggy creatures came bursting upon him. The young soldier pulled his short sword from its scabbard and was about to thrust, when he saw the body beneath the skin. In a sudden flare of the fire, he recognized his mother.

In Calabria, years later, once more Protolcus has fled the crazed outbursts of his fellow human beings. As the light fails upon the hillside, he draws his robes about him, shuddering. He fingers the scar on his left shoulder, the teeth marks of his mother. His mind turns again to the lithesome young virgins, dancing in the firelight, about to be aroused to such pleasure that no man would ever be able to mark them with his passion. Protolcus finds his fingers playing lightly over the strings of his lyre. Below, the rubble of the Chapter House smoulders. He plays the melody of the awful flutes. Under his fingers the melody is softer and more melancholy, but it retains the yearning of the flesh for the touch of flesh.

∵

A few months later, Hippias, elder son of Theolmus, receives a plaintive letter from his father telling of his brother Protolcus' death by suicide. In the same letter, Theolmus asks for news of the "new philosophy," and complains about the resurgence of the Dionysic cult. Hippias is unmoved by the news of his brother's death. He has always thought the boy had inherited their mother's northern madness—in reverse. Hippias grew up with little affection for his family. As soon as he came of age, he cleared out. He settled in Miletus, where he has flourished as a merchant, sending out ships filled with the products of Greek industry to all shores of the world. In return, he receives the rich treasures which his foolish brethren crave. He has become entranced with coins, that invention by which all value is reduced to the measurable quantity of a unit. He marvels at the simplicity of the idea that all coins are exactly alike. Every object on earth can now be valued in common terms.

Carrying the image of his commercial life over into his view of reality, Hippias readily subscribes to the new ideas preached by his neighbors: that a single substance underlies all reality. Commerce thrives on simple relationships, not on confusing ideas of quality and soul. As far as Hippias is concerned, there are only two dimensions to reality: extension and weight. The world is merely the rearrangement of impenetrable atoms, a change in their spatial relationships. The governance of this world requires very simple rules. Those who understand these rules and are able to measure faithfully, will flourish in life. And that is all there is.

Hippias has built himself a palace and lives there alone in great luxury, keeping several women for his pleasure. He gives lavish parties. He has never married. He likes to read his father's letters aloud in the midst of drunken revels. Tonight he acts out a pantomime of his sensitive brother's suicide by hanging with the strings of his own lyre. Overcome with wine and hysterical laughter, the guests seize all of the musicians' instruments, strip them of their strings and walk about with the strings around their necks, eyes wide open and tongues lolling out. Hippias reads aloud his father's attempt to understand the "new philosophy" of the Milesians and the Ionians.

"Dear Son, As you know, I worry more about the way we run our cities than I do about the First Substance. But lately I have been troubled and confused, and I anxiously await correspondence from you for more news about the speculations going on in your part of the world.

"I have just begun to understand what your brother meant when he called you and your friends conservative. Thales, Aniximander and all the rest hark back to the time when there were none of these foolish lustful gods. Zeus came on the scene late, trying to substitute his will and a voluntary contract for the blind force of Destiny and Justice which we call *Moira*.

"I know it must sound ridiculous for me to be thinking about these matters now. Recently, however, we seem on the brink of chaos. If our imagination is to approach the genius of our wives and daughters, we must be brave enough to envision a moral power guiding all of existence, a power without respect for our petty interests, without purpose also, a power which merely portions out the proper boundaries of being, the provinces within which process, nature and growth can function without destroying everything we have built so laboriously.

"Still, as long as there are walls surrounding our lives, and other hands cultivating our vines, digging in our dirt, we will be separated from the prime substance. And then again: Is there a prime substance? And are my walls and the city council and the laws relevant to matter in its purity?

"Since the failure of our reform, and the death of your brother, I grow weary and skeptical about the future. I depend upon you now to awaken my curiosity. I think of you often and hope that you will soon find a wife and begin a family, or, at least, remember your former family. With regret, and much affection, your father."

As he reads the end of the letter, Hippias elaborately wipes imaginary tears from his eyes. He raises his cup in a toast to his father, and to *Moira*, and finally to matter. The assembled company drinks, shouting out a mighty cheer. They live by measurement. They have learned how to chart the distance from land to their precious ships by means of geometry and trigonometry. They keep excellent accounts, using common units of coins to measure, and carefully noted weights.

In the middle of the central wall of Hippias' festal hall stands an immense red marble grave stone with his name exquisitely chiseled on it, along with the following message:

I WAS NOT   I WAS BORN

I AM NOT   IT IS NOUGHT TO ME

TRAVELER FARE YOU WELL

That very night, in a drunken stupor, Hippias drowns in his bath.

A

B   C

D

E

F

G

H

I

J

K

L

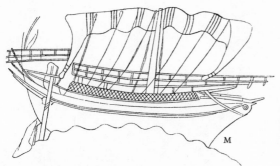

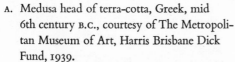

M

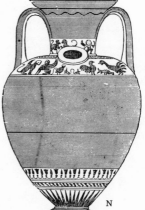

N

A. Medusa head of terra-cotta, Greek, mid 6th century B.C., courtesy of The Metropolitan Museum of Art, Harris Brisbane Dick Fund, 1939.

B. Girl with pigeons, grave relief, Greek, mid 5th century B.C., courtesy of The Metropolitan Museum of Art, Fletcher Fund, 1927.

C. Head of Dionysus.

D. Swords from Attica and Mycenae.

E. Young horseman, marble relief, Greek, 4th century B.C., courtesy of The Metropolitan Museum of Art, Rogers Fund, 1907.

F. Head of an athlete, marble statue, a Roman copy of a Greek work, 5th century B.C., courtesy of The Metropolitan Museum of Art, Rogers Fund, 1911.

G. Dionysus at Sea.

H. Return of Hephaistos to Olympos, escorted by Dionysus, Satyrs and Maenads. Krater, black figured Greek vase of 6th century B.C., courtesy of The Metropolitan Museum of Art, Fletcher Fund, 1931.

I. Greek banquet, vase painting.

J. Early coin of Athens, Greece.

K. Various coins of Greece and Rome, courtesy of The Metropolitan Museum of Art, gift of J. Pierpont Morgan, 1905.

L. View of Olympia, Greece.

M. Greek sailing ship from a vase painting.

N. Greek wine cooler.

VI

Roads Travel
Two Ways

Vitruvius relieved the watch at four in the morning. He was told that the Agrimensor was due just before sunrise, and that he should spruce up because rumor had it that the Architectus himself might very well come to oversee the crucial sighting. This morning the road would take its greatest turn in months: an error of so much as a tenth of a degree would be disastrous. Ahead lay the lowlands full of treacherous swamps. The Pioneer Corps would have to sink piles into the muck and fill the spaces between with great rocks which even now were being quarried in the hill country to the northwest. They would require an immense amount of fill to raise the roadbed the necessary six to eight feet above the floodline. Vitruvius did not look forward to the lowlands—he had already wasted years of his life in the muck. He liked a wide expanse before him.

Vitruvius' own home had been high in the foothills, a countryside of terraces and mountain meadows. From the door of his cottage—the cottage of his father and of his father before him, back generations beyond memory—one could almost make out the sea. He ground his teeth this morning as he did whenever he thought of the land that was no longer his land. Great herds of sheep and cattle, minded by slaves, now trampled his terraces and those of his neighbors. The earth washed down the hillsides, stuffing the gullies, filling the streams; precious soil traveled down to enrich the valley owned by the wealthy landlord who had forced Vitruvius' people off the land. His fellow soldiers had suffered similar fates—all freeholder peasants who had been conscripted and sent to the ends of the Empire to fight great wars, to build forts, walls, and roads. In their leisure, they laid down crops under strange skies while large landholders took possession of their farms and turned the land to pasture for herds of sheep and goats.

Throughout the legions, Vitruvius was known as the "Madman of the Spade," for no one could handle that tool as well as he. Although he had many slaves in his platoon for manual labor, he insisted on launching a job and finishing it with his own hands, making sure that each layer of the roadbed was turned and squared perfectly. He even wielded the spade as a weapon, preferring it to conventional arms. He could brandish it as a sword, a pike, or even a shield; the astonished enemy fell back before his furious onslaughts.

He had been awarded medals without end, only to have them stripped from him. Periodically he would fall into deep depressions and begin to drink. After several days, he would challenge his fellow soldiers, his officers, anyone in sight. If they fled, he would set off straight into the forest, shouting for the enemy to come meet him. He had been broken in rank in every province of the Empire, on all sides of the Mediterranean. Again and again he had been disciplined, but there was always an Architectus who asked for him especially to be part of a new Pioneer Corps. Besides, there were fewer and fewer soldiers every year. The Imperial Power had despoiled the peasantry. Soon there would be no more young men to protect the Eternal Empire.

This morning Vitruvius stood watch in full marching gear: weapons, spade, grain, cookpot, cup, basket, saw, hatchet, sickle and pick. His unit had been ordered to break camp. He might have stacked his gear behind a bush if he were not expecting the Architectus himself. He could be broken in rank if he were discovered out of marching uniform. He enjoyed the little bit of authority he had attained and was tired of losing it for minor infractions.

Vitruvius could never rid himself of a sense of strangeness about his work: the laying of an alien track across the flesh of the earth. Once he had watched a herd of deer come up to a new embankment and stop in utter confusion. The road had been in place only a fortnight. The lead buck circled slowly to assure himself that this was indeed his ancient track to water. He climbed up the embankment and set foot on the stones of the roadway. A few heartier members of the herd followed. Hooves resounding on the slippery stones, the deer took a few steps and then lost their nerve. The buck led his herd back in the direction from which they had come. Watching the retreating beasts, Vitruvius had felt a great sadness. He knew that not far to the east, fellow pioneers of their sister legion were building a similar road, heading north, and that sooner or later, all creatures, animal or human, would be caught in the great Roman net.

As a youth, Vitruvius had felt even worse about road building. Then the memory of his own land had been so strong that he could taste his bitterness. Now he had lived a lifetime on the roads, and even with the strangeness and the sadness and the hatred he felt for the weight of the stones, he had come to love his work too. He had been a farmer, and still planted from time to time, but these days, with each sweep of the spade on the embankment, he felt he was planting even more magnificent seed. Wherever roads went, up would spring towns, wealthy with the produce of the Empire; up would rise fields, richer than any he had seen at home; and out of those fields and towns were spawned a multitude of children. Vitruvius had seen the emptiness filled, the void given shape. He likened his Roman roads to the rivers of God. "Roads are the river courses of man!" he shouted when drunk. And the God who gave them to mankind was the glorious Emperor. He it was who sent out life-giving commerce. Vitruvius himself had added his personal seed to swell the ranks of the Empire's population. Vitruvius had left children along every road he had worked upon, children with his own peculiar talents and madnesses.

Just before dawn the Agrimensor's helpers arrived to set up their instruments. The sighting would be accomplished by aligning a series of red and green lamps. Vitruvius especially liked these sightings in the dark. It seemed to him as if they were ships at sea with port and starboard lights showing. He could already see the lights on the next hill. He imagined the roadway, burying the dark forest which lay like an empty chasm between. At moments like this he was glad that his work brought him to the end of the road. Here were the virginal forests, the austere hillsides and precipitous mountains which would be made to submit to the straightness of Roman Rule.

[91]

Down there in the darkness, enemy bands hid, in gulleys, next to streams, in caves on neighboring hills. Down there animals went about their business, and plants grew just as they had for ages. Streams and forests, swamps and meadows, all unsuspecting, waited the dawn which would bring the great net of Rome over them all.

This was Vitruvius' consolation for the loss of his cottage and his fields. He had extended these roads to the corners of the Empire; these roads defied mountains, rivers, swamps and lakes; these roads cut their straight man-like course across the skin of earth, crying out to the sky: Man has done this thing: Rome, the Eternal City, has tamed the earth.

Vitruvius had been to the capital only once. He had been granted a month's leave to see his family, but when he arrived in his home district, he learned that they had all scattered once their farms had been taken from them. Some cousins, he was told, had gone to Rome to look for work. He never found them. While in Rome Vitruvius had gone to the Forum and spent three days standing in front of the Golden Milestone, reading the distances out loud. Able to read only the numbers, he had to guess at the names. Here was the hub of the wheel which he had spent his lifetime building: All the spokes began and ended here, Rome, the Eternal City, the Sacred City. These roads held in the great Roman net all the lands from the Rhine to the Atlantic, from the Danube and the Black Sea to the Nile, from the Euphrates to the deserts of Africa and the highlands of Britain, three hundred and seventy-two roads, fifty-three thousand miles of great main roads, rural dirt roads, secondary roads, community and gravel roads, causeways, bridges, and incredible tunnels, all fashioned with the hand of Roman genius. For three days Vitruvius marveled, then began to drink. He was picked up two weeks later trying to destroy a tavern near the river.

The Agrimensor and the Architectus arrived at the same time. Both greeted Vitruvius cordially. He had worked with them on many projects. The Agrimensor began his sightings, catching the moment before the first light would make it impossible to see the lamps. Suddenly he let out a curse. The far lights had begun to shake violently, and then they disappeared. Before the Agrimensor's curse had died, Vitruvius, watching the lights, hefted his spade in two hands. He ordered the entire party to retreat immediately. He was just about to send a runner to sound the alarm, when up the sides of the embankment rode a troop with horned helmets, skin shields, and, most frightening of all, long lances mounted to the sides of their saddles. Wild as they looked, they closed ranks in perfect order. Their horses made an incredible clatter on the stones. Below, at the roadhead, the entire woods came alive with lances.

Three of the horsemen turned toward the small surveying party, while a steady flow of horsemen mounted the road, heading south in ranks of four. As the three horsemen approached, Vitruvius, his spade at the ready, stood his ground. The Agrimensor, the Architectus, and the rest of the watch scrambled down into the thick brush by the side of the road where they were slaughtered by a waiting ambush. Before the horsemen reached Vitruvius, a soldier of the watch appeared over the road edge, fleeing the ambush. With a graceful loop, the lead lance dipped and impaled him neatly through the stomach.

Understanding the hopelessness of his plight, Vitruvius dove to the ground and rolled down the embankment until he came to rest in the midst of a thick clump of bushes. For two days he lay unmoving, listening to the clatter of hooves on Roman pavement. Silence returned to the roadhead. Birds sang and beasts rustled through the undergrowth. Vitruvius stood. He removed his insignia and buried them with his arms. Carrying only his spade and seed pouch, he set off through the woods.

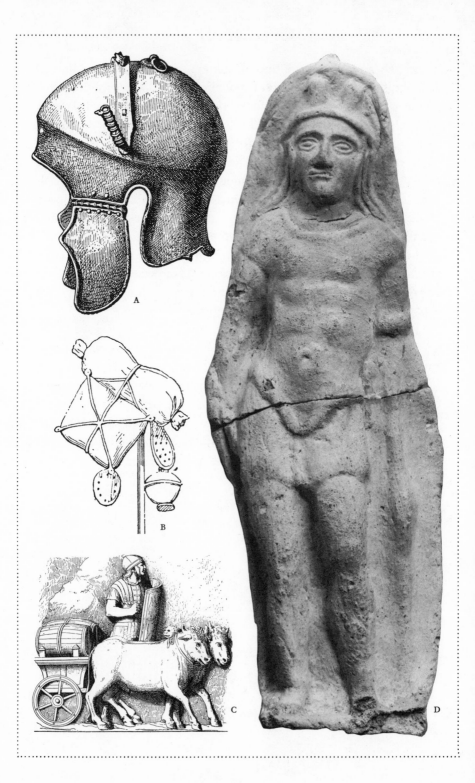

A

B

C

D

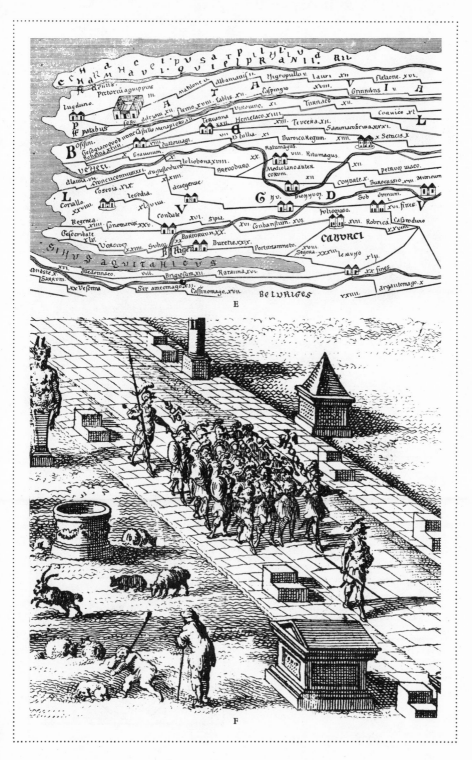

E

F

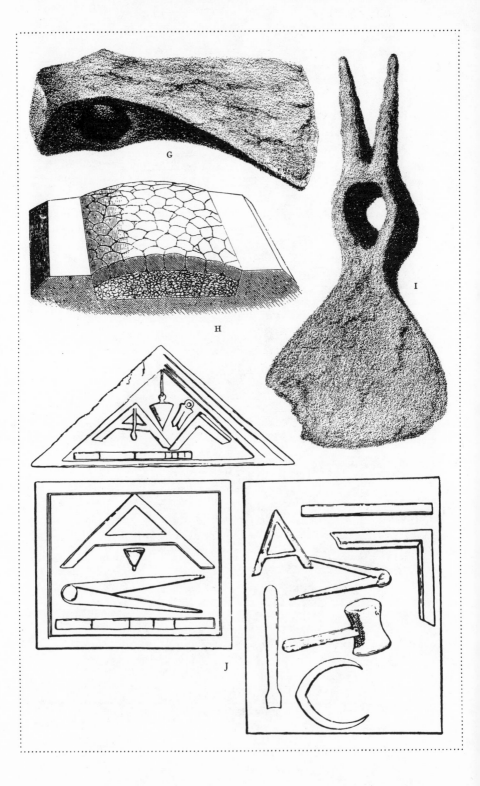

G

H

I

J

A Roman helmet.

B Baggage of a Roman soldier on the march.

C Roman military baggage chariot from a detail in a bas relief of the Trajan Column.

D Gallic soldier, a clay figure from Caere, Italy, courtesy of the Lowie Museum of Anthropology, University of California, Berkeley.

E Western Gaul, a detail from Peutinger's itinerary map of Roman roads, copied from an ancient map by a 13th century monk.

F Roman road from an 18th century woodcut.

G Roman iron axe.

H Cross-section of the paving of an Etruscan road.

I Roman adze, one end for hewing timber, the other for pulling down walls, regular equipment of the Roman legionnaire.

J Tools of Roman masons from tombstones and door-plates, reproduced by permission of the University Museum, University of Pennsylvania.

K Bronze Roman shovel with its handle ending in a ram's horn, courtesy of The Metropolitan Museum of Art, Rogers Fund, 1922.

K

The
Hoop of
Iron

VII
Chernobog's Daughter

At the fair where captives were bought and sold, the bearded German traders, with iron-studded belts around their waists, assembled an odd cargo: giants too large to fit into the holds of Arab ships; wiry, stunted adults; and malformed children whom the Musulmen rejected. All were Slavs, but they had been gathered from lands separated by such distances that they scarcely understood one another's dialects. The men were put to work at the oars. The women and children remained in a clump by the mast, as if that honest spar would provide some security from their captors and the strange craft which carried them so far from their homes. Only one of the captives—a girl-woman—dared to roam the boat freely. She called herself Russalka. The Norse seamen took to her and treated her as a pet.

Even among the strange creatures gathered for this voyage, Russalka had an unearthly look: She was an albino, with dead white hair, lobeless ears, and eyes the color of shallow water over coral. Her pallid skin barely covered the fine skeleton of her bones. Corded tendons and muscles propelled her with agility about the lines and rigging of the ship.

The boat intrigued her. She took great pleasure in all the ship's tackle, and watched every act of the crew with concentration, as if she could learn from their motions how such a large piece of wood moved so gracefully through the water. For hours she leaned down from the bowsprit, concentrating on the point at which the bow cleaved the oncoming water. Sometimes she hung off the stern on a line provided by her sailor friends, undulating through the water like a fish.

Although the German traders and the Norse seamen found the scrawny women captives repulsive and made few sexual advances, the men were attracted to something in Russalka's bearing. Her free movements seduced them, and the candor of her curiosity. She knew how to move about men, climbing on their shoulders, evading their embraces and yet leaving them laughing and delighted as if she were their own curious child. At the same time their cheeks flushed, and in their dreams they found themselves fondling her.

From the beginning of the voyage the other captives had avoided the girl. If she happened to brush against them, they flinched and solemnly recited charms. She took little notice, but when asked her name, she declared it in a loud voice, "Russalka!" provoking a gasp of horror from the other captives. In all Slavic dialects the Russalki were dread water nymphs, born from the souls of drowned maidens. These nymphs were said to seize unsuspecting mortals whenever they ventured too near the sacred rivers, submitting them to terrible tortures as they drowned them. If any of the captives got in her way, Russalka mischievously raised her hands as if to push them into the water. Frightened, they scrambled away, leaving her free to do as she liked.

As the river grew wider, Russalka spent more and more time in her own small nest in the bow, sheltered by the gunwale and the coiled bow lines. Overhead the sky broadened and appeared to descend in the form of a diffused and misty light, permeated with a disturbing smell unlike anything she could remember. Her flesh tingled and the spray left gritty white grains on her skin which tasted sharp and salty.

Now and then she peeked up over the gunwale. The river had almost entirely disappeared. Low swampy shores retreated and then advanced. Up ahead, odd dwarfed trees sprang from the flanks of rocky hills which rose up on either side of the river. Between them was a great gap. As the boat approached the opening, a terrifying rumbling could be heard. The captives cringed. The Norsemen whipped at the oarsmen and tightened their mainsheet. The boat heeled over, driven by a gust of wind. Straight ahead they sailed into a great motionless foaming wave which guarded the gap. Higher and higher they rose, and then leaped forward into a world of light.

"The sea, the sea!" a murmur swept through the captives. Russalka bounded up on the gunwale, perching like a sea bird, knees bent, head high. It was wondrous to behold: so large and empty and fresh. White-caps studded the dark surface, receding to a milky white mist. And then, suddenly, struck with fear, Russalka fell back among the coiled lines, huddling there, staring up at the white sky. In her motionless body, her heart beat rapidly as her mind raced back over the thousands of miles she had traveled. The images of the rapids, the falls, the gorges came painfully clear to her mind. Back and forth she made the journey as if to unravel the distance and the time of this nightmare into which she had been swept from her small village in the wilderness.

When the light had left the sky and dark had descended, slowly she raised herself into a sitting position. Her body ached as if it had followed her mind over all those miles. Stealthily she reached down to the pouch tightly bound around her waist. Loosening the thongs, she ran her fingers over the familiar gnarled root within. She knew the root as she knew her own body; it was alive to her touch.

.·.

Her mother and the land of her birth were far to the east and the south. She had grown up knowing only twenty-three people—her father's family, her mother's, and three other families. They fished and hunted, kept a meager herd of cattle on a meadow, and planted corn in a clearing which they had made themselves when they settled the place. Byelobog ruled the day and Chernobog ruled the night.

Although she had been born an albino, she had not minded being different. "An all-white child for the clear white day," her mother had declared, convincing the village that the child's birth had been marked by Byelobog's favor. Soon everyone loved her and took special care of her. At the annual festival of the god of love, Yarilo, she rode with the maidens on the white cow, garlanded with spring flowers, singing:

> *Where he sets his foot,*
> *The corn grows in mountains;*
> *Wherever he glances,*
> *The grain flourishes.*

[103]

As a small child her favorite goddess was Mati-Syra-Zemlya, Moist-Mother-Earth. She was taught early that Earth was "just" and that one must not deceive her. Whenever a dispute arose, each party placed a clod of earth upon his head and swore his honesty before Earth. Just after the first thaw she used to accompany her father to the fields. He would stand in the center of his plot of ground, a jar of hemp oil on his shoulder. As the first rays of sun touched him, he would speak out four prayers, turning slowly and pouring oil onto the ground from the jar.

To the east: "Moist Mother Earth subdue every evil and unclean being so that he may not cast a spell on us nor do us any harm." To the west: "Moist Mother Earth, engulf the unclean power in thy boiling pits, in thy burning fires." To the south: "Moist Mother Earth, calm the winds coming from the south and all bad weather; calm the moving sands and whirlwinds." To the north: "Moist Mother Earth, calm the north winds and the clouds; subdue the snowstorms and the cold."

When her father finished, he threw the jar to the ground, breaking it. Then he knelt, took up a handful of soil, and bent his ear to it. If he heard the sound of a well-filled sleigh gliding over the snow, his crop would be good, but if the sound was that of an empty sleigh, they would have little to eat that year.

When Russalka grew older she discovered trees. Her parents could not keep her out of the branches. Her small agile body moved about with surprising assurance. In the summer, only her voice could be heard in the thick canopy. As her passion for climbing grew, the villagers began to regard her with less indulgence. It was unnerving to be stalking small game through the forest and suddenly to be startled by a human voice, bearing down from the impenetrable heights. Russalka became more and more mischievous, taking pleasure in her ambushes. And then the river entranced her—the swift, singing river which boiled through the great rocks from the time of the first thaw until the winter freeze.

The villagers were afraid of the river and stayed away from it as much as possible. It had claimed many of their lives. Ponds and streams provided them with adequate water. Even the fishermen traveled for miles to find a more peaceful stretch in which to set their traps. But not Russalka. Day after day, she disappeared from the village, making her way down to the willows hanging over the swiftly running water. All day she swung from the supple limbs, skimming the boiling rapids, mocking the water. Now and then she would let a foot or hand skim through the foam before the limb carried her high above, back into the cool shade. One day the river reached up, seized her body and dragged it out of the trees, tossing it brutally from wave to wave. The river paid her back for her mockery, and for her mischief. Wherever her body moved, sharp stones pummeled her. She was tossed high in the air and she was dragged unmercifully along the bottom.

Two days later a hunter found her stranded on a sandbar. He slung the body over his shoulder to carry it back to the settlement for burial. As he walked, he felt the body twitch and heard a strange gasp. He flung the body down and ran back to the settlement. The whole village returned to find the young girl rocking convulsively in the high grass. The villagers wanted to stone her. The water nymphs had made her their own. If she lived, she would bring evil to the village, luring others to their death in the river. Her mother threw herself upon the child, declaring that she was a child of light. Byelobog had saved her, she shouted, and anyone who dared touch her daughter would be punished. The villagers, afraid of the God of Light, let the child live. But from that time everyone except her parents avoided her. No longer was she welcome at the festival of Yarilo. The other girls of the village chased her away from the white cow and beat her when she tried to deck herself with flowers. They told her that she was Chernobog's daughter now—the daughter of the night.

Abandoned by Yarilo, Russalka switched her affections to Kupala, a fiercer god by far. Kupala was God of Water and of Fire. It was on the eve of the Feast of Kupala that Russalka learned the mysteries of the herbs from her mother. She was eleven years old. She had walked with her mother for miles, farther from the settlement than she had ever gone, following the river at first, and then the course of a mossy stream. Deep in a glen choked with massive old trees, her mother dropped to her hands and knees and began to search in the dark relying on the touch of her fingers. Soon she discovered the fern she sought. It was almost midnight. Three times around the fern her mother drew the magic circle. Then, together they stepped inside. All about them monsters and daemons spoke fair words, tempting them to abandon their quest. With fingers in their ears they squatted, watching the bud climb the length of the stem. At midnight the forest fell silent. Russalka strained her eyes. A great resonant sound rose up from the earth. There before them the bud opened, displaying the delicate flower of the fern. Her mother plucked it: the fern fire-flower. All night the two lay in one another's arms while the trees left the ground speaking among themselves. To her surprise, Russalka understood the words of the trees.

At dawn, her mother showed her how to gather the root of the pla-kune-trayva, the "tear-weed" (purple loose-strife), and then had her repeat the sacred exorcism:

"Tear-weed, tear-weed, thou hast wept much and for a long time, but thou hast gained little. May thy tears not flow in the open field and thy sobs not sound over the blue sea. Frighten wicked daemons, demi-daemons and old witches. If they do not submit to thee, then drown them in thy tears. If they flee from thy glance, engulf them in precipices and pits. May my speech be firm and strong for centuries and centuries."

The morning of Kupala's feast she learned also of the razyv-trayva (saxifrage), "the herb which broke iron, gold, silver and copper," and of the "nameless herb" which allowed one to read the thoughts of others. Afterwards, mother and daughter returned to the village in time to see the women harnessing the wagon. Her mother left her then to join the others. In the forest near the village, the women cut down a tall straight birch, stripped it of all its branches and leaves except for a crown at the top, and carried it back to the meadow. There they placed it firmly in a deep hole and decorated it with wild flowers. The men stayed in their houses until the tree was ready. When the men emerged, they found the figure of Kupala, made of straw and dressed in fine clothes, standing proudly at the base of the birch pole.

All day they danced and sang and ate. At nightfall the sacred fires were lit all about the God and his tall straight birch pole. Men, women, and children leaped over the flames for hours, back and forth. Towards midnight they took up the straw figure of Kupala. Through the high grass they marched, singing mournfully. When they heard the roar of the rapids, they clutched one another. They crept forward until they stood together on the high bank. The most intrepid of their hunters, Kupala on his shoulder, climbed down through the rocks to the river's side. Slowly he lowered his burden into the water. As the waves greedily embraced the God, the voices of the villagers rose in a wail:

"I come to thee, little water-mother, with head bowed and repentant. Forgive me, pardon me—and ye, too, ancestors and forefathers of the water."

They stood thus, chanting for several minutes, and then, with torches held high, they made their way back to camp. No sooner had they entered the clearing than the strange warriors from the north attacked.

∴

For days the ship sailed west along the shore of the great Northern Sea. Whenever they came upon a safe anchorage, they put in to take on fresh water and meat. On one such landing, two Irish monks appeared. In return for passage, the holy men agreed to attempt the conversion of the captives. The conversion took place on that sandy shore in the warm sun of early afternoon. The new Christians were pushed unceremoniously into the outlet of a fresh-water stream while the monks waded about, striking each captive on the forehead or on whatever other part of the body they could reach with their large wooden crosses. Instruction and prayer was left for the monotonous shipboard hours.

For most of the captives, conversion merely meant the addition of a few more gods and heroes to the family. They felt they had entered lands belonging to a foreign king; they were happy to practice the proper forms of obeisance. However, the blow on the forehead by that curious cross and the immersion in water disturbed Russalka profoundly. Her first immersion, that near-drowning in the river near her village, had transformed her from a child of the Day to a child of the Night. Nor would she forget the last time she had seen her favorite god, Kupala, committed to the torrent—the night the raiders struck, burning her village and taking her captive. Now these two creatures, monks in their odd cowled robes, told her that she had been blessed by the water and bound to the One all-powerful God in the sky, who would gather the good to his bosom after death and cast the evil ones down below. This God she identified as Byelobog, the God of Day. The terrible angel who wished to pull them all into his fires could be none other than

Chernobog, God of Night. But Russalka was Chernobog's daughter. Was she then the daughter of Satan?

Dreams of water and fire tortured Russalka in the weeks after her conversion. She cried in the night when no one could see her. She was convinced that somehow she had entered the lands ruled by the root, plakune-trayve, the "tear-weed." They were sailing over the blue sea of the incantation, and doubtlessly she was surrounded by wicked daemons, demi-daemons and old witches. Feeling that her own sinewy body was sister to that hard root in her pouch, she prayed for the root to drown the evil spirits in her tears. Grasping the root for comfort, she fell asleep at last.

The nights became cold, and the days cloudy. Autumn filled the air. Storms swept in from the sea, battering their boat, making it difficult to proceed. Several of the weaker captives fell ill and began to cough. Russalka boiled an herb tea which they inhaled and then drank. They rested more easily. One of the monks, the fat one, now came secretly to the girl for help with running sores which covered his lips. While she examined him, he held up his cross between them. Russalka understood the gesture and was offended. Had he not converted her to his God? She too was protected by the crucified man on the cross.

Although Russalka did not know how to treat the monk's illness, she was too clever to admit her ignorance. Instead, she gathered some innocuous herbs, ground them up and made a paste with water and the gum of trees, spreading it over the sores. On the dressing she caked mud, all the while mumbling nonsense words. Pleased with her gentle ministrations, the monk blessed her. He even let her hold his cross, and asked her to repeat some of his odd Latin words. One of his hands crept up between her legs. Seized by a spirit of mischief, Russalka slipped away from him and went running about the boat, waving the cross, swinging from lines and leaping over stanchions while the monk chased her about.

Perched high upon the mast, Russalka examined the cross with care. There upon the worn wood was carved the crude figure of the young crucified god. She could even make out the holes in the arms and legs. She peered into the figure's face to see whether he was Yarilo or Kupala, but he looked like neither. As she gently stroked the tortured body on the cross, she remembered the terrifying attack upon her village on the night of Kupala's feast. Blood and screams filled her memory. She thought now of the willow branches over the river on which she had swung and remembered the water clutching up at her; she thought of her dear father blessing Moist-Mother-Earth and the angry faces of the girls who chased her away from the white cow of Yarilo. Now she touched the root in her pouch with her other hand, and a strange feeling rose within her. She began to rock back and forth, moaning, unable to understand these confused memories. Weeping, Russalka inched down the mast and handed the cross back to the monk who stalked off petulantly. The girl fled forward to her nest in the bow.

∵

By the time the captives had become accustomed to the rhythms of the Northern Sea, the boat turned into the delta of a river far grander than the one by which they had entered the sea. Beating against a powerful current, the Norsemen had need of all the power they could get from their oars. Women and children were put to work. Russalka threw all of her weight into the new task, happy to be free of her brooding thoughts for a while. On the second day up the river, the captives were amazed by what they saw. On either shore, wide, flat, cultivated plains stretched out for miles. Wherever they looked, they could make out small settlements of well-built cottages. The captives had never seen so many settlements, so many people living close to-gether on the land. They could not understand how the thick moist soil of the bottomland had been made to bloom. The trees themselves had retreated, leaving only tokens of resistance in copses which here and there separated one farm from another.

Russalka could not wait to step on land, to feel the earth in her hands. Several times during the day she caught sight of men ploughing in the distance. The ploughs were enormous, with wheels, pulled by teams of two, four, and sometimes six oxen. She might have thought she was dreaming, had not her companions seen the same miraculous sights. None could understand why they were ploughing so late in the year.

Before dusk fell the second day, the craft rounded a bend in the river and came to a sweeping beach. No sooner had the captives helped pull the boat high on the gravel shore than they were herded by strange guards, without ceremony, up over the embankment and through the lanes of an immense settlement. Russalka kept craning her head to catch a glimpse of that miraculous craft which had carried her so far over the surface of the earth, but it had disappeared in a moment, just as her own home had vanished on the night of the raid. In her hand she grasped the pouch with her roots and herbs. She felt abandoned by her new God and his servants, the Irish monks, the German traders, and the Norse seamen.

Early in the morning, before dawn, the captives were awakened and fed a thin soup. The guards herded them out onto a wide muddy track which led off between the fields towards the west. As she walked, Russalka kneaded a clod of muddy soil between her hands. The light ploughs used by her people would never have been able to turn this soil. Bottomlands were always left to the forest and the river. As day broke behind the scraggly troop, Russalka peered out into the fields hoping for a glimpse of the machines which had accomplished this gigantic task. Now she could make out the furrows, long low ridges, like waves running in strips over the wide plain. Shortly, the troop came abreast one of the earth machines being pulled by four oxen and directed by a thick-set young man. The farmer hailed the guards, asking for news. While the guards and the farmer chatted, Russalka crept through the hedgerow and began to examine the plough. She had never seen anything more beautiful and intricate and strong. The light ploughs her people used scarcely tickled the surface of Mother Earth, but this monster delved deep into her rich interior. One metal knife dug straight down, while the second cut the earth horizontally at the grass roots, and the wood board flung the turned earth to one side, like the bow of a boat through water.

Russalka knelt in the ploughed surface of the field, picked up the rich crumbling loam in her hands, and cried out to the "just" Earth: "I did nothing to cause the strangers to attack my people. I am no water daemon. Please deliver me from this shame. Return me to my people and my rightful place, for I worship you, Moist-Mother-Earth, Mati-Syra-Zemlya."

Just then the farmer turned back to his plough. Discovering the odd little creature kneeling in the field, he called out to the guards. They came to retrieve her, beating her back to the track with their staffs. Russalka bore the half-hearted beating stoically, keeping her eyes upon the retreating farmer, and the thick clots of earth tossed to the right of the plough as it proceeded through the earth. She could feel those sharp metal blades cutting into the flesh of Moist-Mother-Earth, blades larger than any she had ever before seen. Her own people used iron, but only in a small way. These bearded Germans had found some great secret source for such wonderful implements, she thought.

For two days they proceeded on the slowly rising track before they reached a forest. Carts of all sizes and shapes passed them, pulled by donkeys, oxen, horses; warriors on horseback carrying great iron swords and lances brushed by.

Within the forest, the track rose and fell. The captives had now passed into a region of hills, with ravines on either side, and streams cutting out deep gulleys. Just before nightfall on the second day the forest ended. And yet, it did not end. Where trees should have been standing, there were only stumps—as if a violent wind had swept up all the trees, or a great fire had cleared the land. Russalka remembered the night when the trees had wandered about the magic circle talking among themselves while she and her mother lay in one another's arms. These trees had departed the land permanently, leaving stumps and roots behind. The guards made camp at the edge of the wasteland, and the captives huddled together fearfully. Russalka stayed apart till darkness fell, but then she too crept among her fellow Slavs for comfort.

The next day as they followed the track, they began to hear strange sounds in the distance: two voices, a deep bellowing roar and a high, intermittent ringing, like that of a deadened bell. Dawn had not yet broken when the troop came to a steep descent. Patches of ground fog, ghostly white, rose in wisps towards them. At the end of the valley before them they could see the outcrops of rocky hills and beyond them the dim shapes of mountains bathed in moonlight. All along the base of the hills, at intervals, burned brilliant fires, brighter than any the girl had ever seen. As they descended into the valley, dawn came.

With the rising of the sun, they approached a large settlement of buildings. The bellowing and ringing deafened them. At last the western hillsides became clearly visible. Now Russalka understood where the trees had gone. Strange constructions of wood flowered over the hills as far as she could see. High ladders climbed the precipices. Beams, swinging from lines, were carried into yawning chasms which had been dug out of the sides of the cliff walls. All along the crest, odd-shaped scaffoldings rose at intervals. It looked as if men were trying to cram the entire forest into the mountainside. Farther north Russalka could make out whole mountains which had been dug out and abandoned.

The giants cut and hauled trees, prepared them for shoring, and hammered at the forges; the dwarfs and children plunged into the dark world of the shafts, crawling, wriggling, slithering like serpents through the narrow passageways. The labor within the mines was hard, monotonous and unremitting. Twelve, fourteen, sixteen hours a day they chipped away at the precious veins, tugging and hauling the crumbled fragments of ore back towards the flaming furnaces and the singing forges at the foot of the precipices. The world seemed to have an endless appetite for iron. Like the other children, Russalka spent her first months serving as a messenger and a beast of burden, dragging baskets almost as heavy as she along the smooth plankways to the crude wagons which awaited. She was always cold. Half the time, ground water lapped at her ankles. She entered the mines in the dark, and left them in the dark; time and light disappeared. Sometimes whole shafts flooded suddenly, drowning everyone within. Now and then a spark ignited explosions of mine-damp, caving in sections of the galleries. It seemed that every day the wails and screams of the lost and buried echoed dimly through the shafts towards the light.

Miraculously, Russalka always sensed impending disaster and managed to save herself. At first she was tempted to imitate some of her comrades who, out of fear of the dark confinement, chose deliberately to die. But she could not bring herself to surrender to the doubts which tormented her. She felt that one day she would unravel the mystery of Christ, of Byelobog, of Chernobog, Satan, Kupala, fire and water. She blamed no one for her plight. She could see that her masters were driven as hard as she. "Iron, more iron," thundered the furnaces.

Waiting at the nether end of the shafts for the miners to dislodge enough ore to fill her basket, she watched their motions with care. She examined their tools: a broad shovel of iron and wood; a pickaxe of iron, sixteen inches long, sharpened at one end and flat-headed at the other to drive iron wedges or chisels into the cracks of the rock. She saw a miner choose a fault in the rock and hammer in his chisel. If he chose the correct fault, the entire rock would shatter. When that happened, Russalka felt an intense pleasure warm her breast. Some miners were clever, but most tried many times before they succeeded.

One day she stopped a clumsy young miner who was fruitlessly hammering at a solid rock wall. She stroked the rock face, she lay her cheek upon its cold surface and held her lamp up close. It seemed as if Chernobog himself spoke to her. She touched the root, crumbled now in her pouch. It knew where treasure lay buried. She ran her hand over the rock face and pointed to an almost invisible cleft. The miner placed the chisel and tapped it into place. Then he took a mighty swing and the entire rock crumbled, almost crushing the two of them. The next day, the miner let her hold the chisel, and within two weeks Russalka had become a miner herself.

At first the young woman found joy in her new duties. She loved the tools she wielded and fondled them when she was not at work. Her unerring pick had a way of prying out the purest ores which came from the mines. The smiths respected this talent, a magic akin to their own. Russalka liked to stand near the furnaces and forges, watching while the rough formless ore was roasted with charcoal and a flux, marveling at the tough spongy bloom of iron covered with liquid slag collecting at the bottom of the furnace. Again the bloom was reheated, luminous as the petal of a flower in sunlight, and she thrilled to the hammer blows which drove out all the slag, leaving the pure precious substance to be shaped.

The smiths formed an exclusive group. Beneath their forges they buried strange fetiches. Their struggle to separate out the iron was considered a wresting of God's treasure from its rightful place. This idea disturbed the young woman. At night she fell asleep, questioning her own labor deep within the womb of Moist-Mother-Earth. A terrifying shadow stalked her sleep. But why? The mystery of the Gods remained.

Day after day, as Russalka labored in the mines, a question grew in her mind concerning the ore. Unlike the grains of her father's fields, or the trees of the forests, or even the waters of the rivers, the ore was never replenished. On Sundays, when she did not work, she sometimes explored the worked-out mines to the north, crawling down into the galleries which had not yet been stripped of their buttressing. This way and that, she cast her lantern beam to see if there were any signs that the veins of iron had begun to grow again. The mines remained as they had been left: stripped of their riches. When she asked the miners and the smiths where the iron had come from, they always pointed down towards the center of the earth. The young woman wondered if she would ever break through into that nether realm and discover the great furnaces of Chernobog.

Iron became for Russalka the final concentrated form of all the mystery of the universe which had torn her from her land and had carried her to this devastated place. On her day out of the mines, she wandered over the countryside, unable to enjoy the sky, the streams, or the green growing plants. Instead, she thought about the rich veins of metal wealth beneath her feet—treasures which one day soon, she would plunder. Silent and morose, Russalka returned to camp. One day, she did not appear at her place in the shafts, nor could she be found throughout the camp. At first the matter was kept quiet—the foreman did not want to employ the brutal camp soldiers who were merciless to escaped slaves. Secret search parties were sent out into the wilds all about, but no trace of the girl could be found. One of the smiths remembered that Russalka had been in the habit of returning to the mined-out shafts. At the end of a deep shaft, the young woman was found unconscious, suffering from a high fever. The smiths tended her, allowing no one near. They chanted their mysterious prayers and applied herbal remedies.

In her crazed illness, Russalka found herself carried back along the wide river, back across the Northern Sea, back through the sinuous river, over the land, through swamp and forest to her village. There she stood, a child again, by her father, in the midst of his field. With the jar of hemp oil on his shoulder, he turned to the east, addressing Moist-Mother-Earth: "Subdue every evil and unclean thing so that *she*"—here he pointed at the child—"may not cast a spell on us nor do us any harm! Engulf *her* unclean power in thy boiling pits, in thy burning fires!" With horror, Russalka saw her beloved father slowly pour the

[114]

oil over the head of the albino child standing trustfully at his side. Choking and sputtering, the child cried out and ran towards her mother who crouched against a giant fern in fear, warding the child off with the sacred root. The white-haired child stopped short, anger filling her body, melting its outlines. The body became a mist which danced like a flame about the crouched and wailing woman, trying to consume her. "Drown the wicked daemon in thy tears," shouted out her beloved mother, waving plakune-trayva all about. "Engulf *her* in thy precipices and pits." Now a wind blew at the wavering mist of the white-haired child-daemon, filling it like a sail, blowing it through a long winding course among trees to a cliff where a yawning black hole swallowed it.

After two days, Russalka awoke. She lay perfectly still for some time in her pallet in the smiths' quarters. For the first time since the terrible night of Kupala's feast when her village had burned, she felt at peace with herself. She knew now that she was the "evil and unclean being," "the daemon" against whom her parents chanted their prayers. The "tear-weed" had conjured up the Norsemen, the Irish monks, and the Germans to purge her from the pure wilderness of her village and carry her to the dark chasms and flames of the mines. Chernobog had become Satan and had condemned her to this "hell" of which the monks, with their high-pitched mewling voices, had warned.

Curiously, once Russalka accepted this knowledge, her torment ended. At last she had found her rightful place. No one could accuse her of usurping the realm of light. How could they threaten her? She had survived death and had passed into a living realm of the Lord of Darkness. Feeling as if she had awakened from the dream of Life, she recovered. Now she entered the dim narrow passageways singing. She breathed in deeply, savoring the damp dusty air which gave substance to the darkness. The dancing shadows became her beloved companions. Occasionally she paused to embrace the crystalline shapes carved in Earth's rocky womb. As the days passed she began to pity her parents and all those who walked the surface of Moist-Mother-Earth, all those who depended upon Her whim and caprice for their livelihood. She, Russalka, had been sucked into the Moist Mother's body and had become one with Her power. To Russalka, daemon nymph, had been granted the freedom to wander through the source of all waters, the nurturing house of seeds and roots, the storehouse of the great fires of the sun and the treasure house of the precious ore.

In her new-found contentment, Russalka allowed herself to be wooed and won in marriage by the strongest of all the smiths. When she was not bearing children, she continued to go down into the mines. She told her children that one day humans would discover the place where Chernobog replenished Earth's stock of ore.

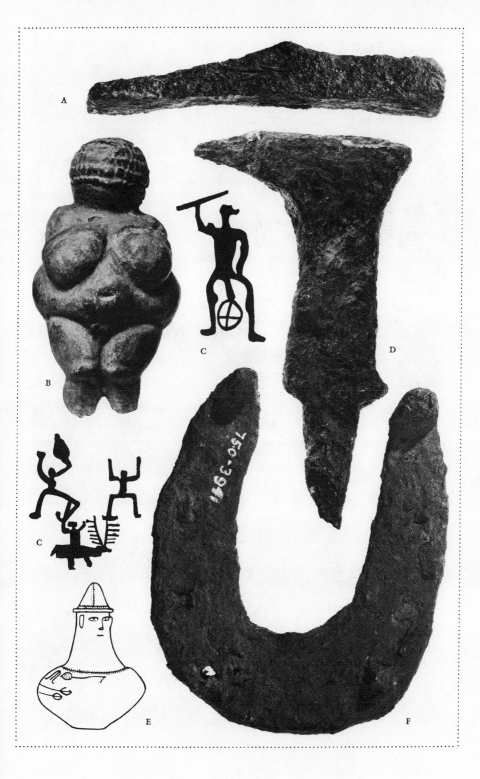

A

B

C

D

C

E

F

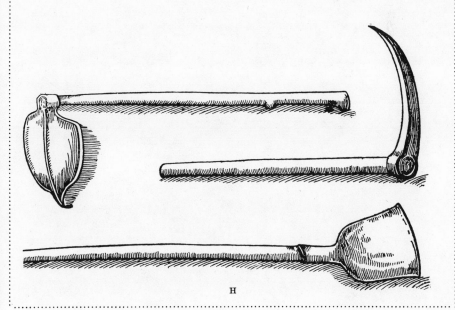

H

VIII
Stirrup and Soil

THE monks and the priests are always telling us about the power of God. They assure us that this whole new order of things comes with God's blessing. They want us to accept everything and get on with our main work, which is to prepare for the next world. I'm as concerned as anyone about that other life, but I can't help wondering about this one. Of course, it is possible that God wanted to make a statement about our earthly life, and that he chose a simple lowly object with which to make that statement. It doesn't entirely fill me with confidence to think that everything has changed because of two oblong metal rings at the end of hide thongs. These two rings have revolutionized the way we men and women treat one another; they have degraded our brotherhood with the land, and they have dictated the future of our children and grandchildren. Because of these two absurd items, some of us have become masters while others have become slaves. Slave is perhaps too mean a word, and master too grandiose. But the relationship which the priests insist upon—that of father and child with responsibility towards one another—is not entirely accurate either.

Our village is a backwater. No one comes this way unless he is related to one of the families hereabouts. The two great bishoprics which lay claim to most of our land make their headquarters in a distant province. Now and then a messenger appears from one or another asking a tithe of their land. Generally we get away with giving them very little. The King's palace is even farther away. When a messenger arrives from the palace, the problem is more serious, because it means the loss of our best young men. We are loyal Franks, however, and stalwart warriors. Our village heroes have always helped advance the cause of our tribe. We understand that the recent kings of the Franks have not been particularly able or strong men. The power of the tribe has generally been wielded by the Mayor of the Palace and the nobles. We ourselves have avoided these modern developments. We still govern ourselves in the old way: family, clan, and the King. We are all freemen in the village and farmers. When we need leaders at war or to settle disputes, we choose them by acclamation. At war, the best fighters take the lead, but at home others are given authority for their wisdom.

All this, of course, was true before the time of the two oblong metal rings. These ingenious, mean little objects made their appearance at our village on a day seemingly no different from any other day. A band of men were seen approaching the village, led by three horsemen. Our first thought was that we would be losing young men to war once again. But as the troop came closer, we were amazed to see an incredible figure on the lead horse, all wrapped in iron, his two feet firmly placed in two oblong metal contraptions attached to either side of the most elaborate saddle we had ever seen. On one arm he carried a large metal shield, and in the other he held a long lance such as none of us had ever seen before. Near the top of the lance was a cross-piece, and from it fluttered a pennant. The colors of the pennant were not those of our King.

Abandoning our ploughs, we ran for our weapons. However, before the band reached our farthest field, the metal creature on horseback lifted the visor of his helmet to show the wise gray head of one of the renowned captains of the King. In days of old, a few of us had fought under his command in certain local wars. Still clutching our weapons, we went to meet the visitors. The good captain laughed at our caution and at our amazement. We began to laugh in return. Curious, we crowded around touching the saddle, knocking the armor, examining the cunning fastenings of this novel equipment. Within a moment, the two other horsemen had pulled up on either side of the Captain, rudely brushing us back. In spite of the Captain's protestations, the two horse-men herded us to the side of the track, and our tempers flared. The Captain issued a curt command, however, and his lieutenants reluctantly backed away. Another command brought three footmen forward on the run, one with a stool. At the same time, two other footmen took the reins of the lieutenants' horses. We expected the Captain to dismount immediately, helped by the three footmen. Instead, he waited until his lieutenants had dismounted and had come around to help him down. A complicated order ruled those who touched the Captain, those who held his horse, and so on. All these new manners filled us with apprehension. Now a whole crowd surrounded the Captain, removing helmet, heavy breastplate, shield and sword, scurrying about him like bees caring for the queen bee. We of the village found it embarrassing to watch one man treated with such attention by his fellows, each one intent upon winning his favor. We stood across the track, dumbfounded, shifting from foot to foot, and giggling behind our hands. We knew we were behind the times, but if we hadn't recognized the Captain, we might have thought these visitors to be moon men. Now the crowd parted, and the Captain stepped towards us wearing garments more beautiful than any we had seen before. Without hesitation he took up our reluctant hands. He spoke familiarly, in the rude vernacular of the countryside, and soon we felt compelled to offer him hospitality. Ordinarily, visitors were invited to share the warmth of our own huts for the night, even if it meant that we slept with the animals. Today we made the gesture, although we could not imagine anyone so dressed sleeping in our pallets. The Captain politely declined and asked permission to pitch his tent on the flat near the spring.

He seemed in no particular hurry to discuss the matter which brought him to this out of the way place. Instead, he walked with us through our village, considerately inquiring after our crops, our families, and the like. He asked a number of questions about the bishoprics and their demands on us. We began to fret that the church would want past tithes which we had so conveniently omitted all these years. Later it occurred to me that we were under no obligation to answer his questions, nor to give him more than a stranger's hospitality. We had a certain duty to our King, when he called upon us to do battle, but as for his captains, they were simply fellow Franks. More than one of our own past heroes had been a captain to past kings of the Franks. Still, the respect and obedience which his own men showed to this man proved seductive. We found ourselves bowing now and then and seeking to help the Captain avoid ditches and ordure, as if we had joined his entourage. But more than one of us caught ourselves and drew back, and, with the others, made fun of the grand manners which the Captain seemed to have learned since last we saw him on the battlefield.

As was customary whenever respectable strangers appeared in our obscure village, we had a feast that night out of doors. We set up the large trestle table which we reserved for that purpose. Each man brought his own stool. The Captain sat on a most intricately shaped chair of fine polished wood, a chair which folded up flat for traveling. The chair amazed us almost as much as the armor, the saddle, and the rest of the funny business surrounding the Captain. After we had all eaten and drunk a considerable amount, the Captain began to tell us about the Moors.

The shrewdest among us began to understand that great changes were in the wind. We heard about the dark-skinned people who had spread across the world to the south of the great Southern Sea, and then had leaped across its mouth up into the western provinces. Our warriors had brought back tales of great battles, cruel piracy at sea, and of the new religion which these peoples had founded in our very own Christian book. None of us had ever seen a Musulman or a Moor, nor did we ever expect to see one. When he said that the dark-skinned armies already had crossed over into the Frankish kingdom, we laughed as children, so improbable did the story seem. He became angry at our laughter and began to describe what such evil dark men did to the women and children of their enemies. He called forth one of his people who had ventured out of Frankish land, down into the western provinces to fight as a mercenary. This man recounted tales of the great bravery and cruelty of these creatures of Mohammed.

"They are coming this way," said the Captain, in stern decisive voice. "They are men with belief—they fight to the death for their Allah and for his prophet."

He then told us details of this enemy's method of battle. First the mounted bands of raiders swept down upon unprotected settlements like ours, putting the men to the sword, raping the women and carrying a few back as slaves after setting everything to the torch, including the fields. Afterwards, when the main armies had made contact, there would be a wild charge of the Berber tribesmen, once captives and now allies of the Arabs. Mounted on swift steeds, shouting allegiance to their god and prophet, they would sweep across the battlefield like a scythe through a field. If the opposition held, the horsemen fell back slowly, battling all the while, gathering up wounded. Joyfully, the opposing army would follow, certain of having broken the enemy's spirit. Then, just when it seemed as if the Franks were to destroy the forces of Allah, an even more violent counterattack would come from reserves. If the Franks did not panic at this second wild attack, the battlefield became the stage for an awesome spectacle. The enemy trumpets would blast and the entire Arab host would march forward slowly, in close formation—with even lines, like worshippers. Indeed, as they marched they chanted prayers in unison. By now they would have demoralized the Franks and would sweep to a complete and devastating victory.

After delivering this solemn portrait of the triumph of the Musulman hosts, the Captain rose and courteously excused himself, thanking us for our hospitality. He and his men made their way to their gorgeous tents, down by the spring, and we could hear them laughing and talking late into the night. There was one who played the lyre and sang a haunting song of death in battle. Then there was silence, and our own restless dreams of the coming tide of dark foreign bodies who would take our land and people it with their Allah-worshipping kind.

The next day we went to our fields early as usual, and found, to our astonishment, the visitors were up too. After their breakfast, they moved to the back meadow, which was free of beasts now, and began to practice feats of war. There was swordsplay, archery, wrestling and the like. One by one we abandoned our ploughs and drifted over to watch. Finally the Captain appeared. Dressed in his armor, he was assisted up onto his horse. A straw dummy swung from the branches of the great oak, attached with three long ropes. Now the Captain charged, lance lowered, braced against the side of the saddle. The lance entered the dummy mid-chest, struck the cross-piece, and carried the dummy back fifteen feet. The impact was great. We fully expected the Captain to fall from his horse, but instead we saw his feet surge against the iron hoops which hung from the saddle. He remained firmly sitting on his horse. We were dumbfounded. Here was a great machine of war. No matter how skillful the Berber horsemen were with their great curved swords, they would never reach the flesh of our warriors. These lances so firmly anchored to horse and saddle would sweep them from their mounts. And even if they evaded the lances, the heavy armor would foil the destructive blades.

Now the Captain reined in his mount and reared it backward, able to disengage the lance easily because it had only penetrated up to the cross-piece. We marveled at the simplicity of this device which would free our lancers to charge once more. While we cheered, the Captain made several more passes at the dummy. His lieutenants manipulated it back and forth with the guy ropes. When the Captain had finished, he rode over to the stone wall where we were sitting. With the help of his re-tainers he dismounted and sat in the folding chair, facing us.

"If there are thousands of Berbers on horseback, how many of us must there be, wearing armor, carrying this lance? And where shall our King find these warriors?" We had no idea. There were very few horses in the area. They cost too much to buy, let alone maintain. And the saddle, the lance, the armor? Besides, where would anyone find five people to dress him, help him on and off the horse, and do all the other services necessary? "Then shall we bow to the Musulmen and give them our wives and children as slaves? And what of the Magyars, and those other wild people pressing from the East?" We stared stupidly at our visitor. He rose and once more courteously excused himself. As he walked away, he turned and added, "The Arab armies have been sighted massing as far north as Gascony. We think they are about to cross the Loire and besiege Autun."

He was subtle, our Captain was. He did not hurry our country minds. He merely fed them every few hours with a few more terrible facts. The vision of Musulmen besieging one of our own cities was beyond imagining. Autun was deep within our land. No one had told us that the dark-skinned nation had even crossed our borders, and now we were asked to believe that a third of our lands were under their control.

That evening at our second festive meal, the Captain informed us that in order to protect the lands of the realm, the King had asked the Church to grant benefices to the great warriors of the realm. He, the Captain, had been given all these lands to protect—our lands, he meant, the lands we have been farming for generations. "I do not own the land," he was quick to point out, "nor your persons. I have merely been granted the fruit of the land in order to protect it for the common good."

This was a difficult idea for us to absorb. I doubt if any of us really understood the legal and philosophical aspects of the matter. We did understand, however, that we were now the Captain's men. "Unless, of course," he continued, "you do not desire protection." Discreetly, he did not mention that should we refuse his offer, we would be obligated to move somewhere else.

That was quite enough to absorb for one evening. We hoped the Captain would take another one of his elegant departures and let us spend the night thinking. Unfortunately, he was not so inclined. Having gone this far, he went all the way.

"My castle is not near enough to your settlement for me to provide you with immediate succor from marauding bands. Therefore, I am going to be generous with you. I will grant you the right to support your own defender. One of you shall don armor which I have brought along, mount his own horse, and carry the lance, bearing my colors. He shall be my liege man. And when the call comes to confront the Musulman, he and all the other liege men of the realm will join with the liege lords in the mightiest army ever to face the paynims! Tomorrow morning I want the decision of your council, for we must tailor the armor and teach the man the rudiments of his new trade."

Ahh, if it had not been for those infernal oblongs of iron, all would have remained the same. One man would not have become different from any other man, just as all crows are equal to all other crows, all woodpeckers like to all other woodpeckers. It was one thing to see the Captain, whom few of us knew, become one of such a different species that we hardly knew how to speak to him, but now we were asked to make one of our own join into an entirely different order—as if the crows were asked to choose one of their kind to become an eagle.

We still find it difficult to talk about this time. The change occurred so simply, without much fuss or bother. What the Captain said made good sense. Our enemies were strong. We had the capability to be stronger: stirrups, saddle, lance, and armor. And yet when we came together in council, even the wisest among us trembled. We knew that we were about to make a change in the natural order. We were about to create a new species out of our own kind. And indeed, the consequences proved even more extreme than we guessed, for lifting one man up on a horse resulted in pushing many men and women down. And the land, the soil which had been our mother, now became a pledge in the lottery of war and violence. The land whose bounty had kept us free men now enslaved us. It mattered little whether the slavery was safe and comfortable, or whether it was harsh and oppressive. Contracts were about to be made over our heads which would bind us for countless generations.

As for our choice, it turned out to be one none of us could have wished. There were only two adequate horses in the settlement. One belonged to the widow Marguerite, a shrewd and bitter woman who had driven her husband to his grave with her greed. And the other belonged to the good-natured Luc. A horse was left to him by his father, our late smith, because Luc had learned to do scarcely anything else than ride wildly about the countryside. Luc's older brother had inherited the smithy, and his younger brother took over the farm after Luc had almost ruined it by his ignorance. Everyone always said it was a pity there were no wars, because Luc was only fit to be a soldier. He was brave, daring even. And he was a good hunter, although he tended to overdo matters, coming back with much more than was needed. Of course, we could have pooled our funds and bought the two horses, and then invested them in one of us, the natural leaders of the settlement. But we were either too old, or too weak; we had no taste for the prospect of charging down upon Berber horsemen. There was another element to the situation too. None of us could quite make the leap of imagination necessary to sit so high above the others. We were modest men, and to become a liege man and a liege lord in the new order offended some innate sense of right. Luc probably would not have made that leap either—in spite of the fact that his eyes glowed when he watched the Captain prancing about in his ridiculous suit of armor, waving the lance at the straw dummy. However, the widow Marguerite understood the situation better than any of us. She got to Luc the afternoon of the council meeting, and by the time we had all sat down to discuss matters, she informed us that she and Luc were about to be married. Thus Luc would not only own the only two adequate horses, he would have a substantial farm, the produce of which would form his contribution to the upkeep of our new warrior troop. His brother, the smith, would prove invaluable in maintaining his arsenal, and his other brother, the farmer, would add to his provisions and to those of his mounts.

Now began the village politics. We all had sons who would need to go to war. Whoever rode closest to Luc would raise his family up. And so the widow Marguerite began to sort out the matter in a series of private conversations, coming away from each with a little more of what she had wanted over these years—a portion of an orchard, some first rate seed, money even—it took one's breath away to see how efficiently that lady put her new position to work in the way of material goods. By the next morning when Luc was to put on armor for the first time—the smith had stayed up all night altering it for his brother—Luc had the necessary retinue to help him dress, to carry his stool, to care for his horse, and to accompany him to the wars.

Obligingly the Captain and his men instructed Luc and his new entourage on the niceties. It was not until shortly before noon that Luc was ready to mount, fully clothed in his armor. Once again we were dismayed that the colors on Luc's lance were not those of our natural leader, the King, but those of the Captain.

During the entire morning, Luc played the fool, strutting, complaining about the stiffness of his limbs, butting his helmet against the oak, and trying to embrace the village girls who easily ran away from him. As the hour to mount grew near, he turned silent and thoughtful. His voice sharpened slightly when a boy tripped over his lance. He refused to mount his horse until the stool carrier came forward, and even then raised a fuss because the stool had not been placed with the correct flourish. Then he waved everyone away except for his two chief aides, whose families had paid dearly for the privilege.

After much huffing and puffing and two or three embarrassing slips, Luc got up into the saddle and tucked his feet safely into the stirrups. When he found himself firmly in place, he sat quite comfortably. We all stood around looking up at this ironclad figure, sitting straight upon the elaborate saddle, lance held high with one arm, and the other hand

[129]

clasping the reins. It was no longer our familiar Luc up there; it was a creature of another order. The horse pranced two steps to the right, and two steps to the left. Luc rode the saddle like an experienced sailor in his skiff. For all his failings, Luc was a superb athlete. In spite of the unfamiliar trappings, Luc's horse recognized his master and bore the rattling and clanking with equanimity. The strangers were quite impressed. They had visited other villages where the chosen champions had not acquitted themselves nearly so well.

Now the Captain joined Luc. The two warriors trotted amiably about the meadow. They went through a number of exercises before performing a mock battle. We all applauded and cheered, proud of our champion. When Luc descended from his horse, his retainers leaped to their appointed tasks with great alacrity. Young men who had been Luc's familiar companions just yesterday, became his willing servants.

After Luc's helmet had been removed and his sword taken away, he knelt before the Captain, placing his hands in the Captain's, and made a pretty little speech affirming his intention to serve the Captain for life against all men. We had never heard Luc speak so well, and we fell back, a touch of fear in our hearts. The Captain raised Luc to his feet and kissed him on the mouth. Now one of the lieutenants brought forth a bible from the tent. With his hand on the bible, Luc swore complete loyalty and fidelity to the Captain.

Although we did not move a step further, we felt the distance grow between us and the principals in that ceremony on our common meadow. In full view of the great noon sun, the Captain bent over, took up a handful of our soil, and placed it in Luc's hand.

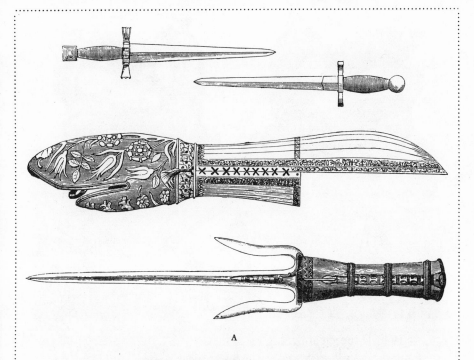

A

HUYOT

B

C

D

E

A Moorish arms.

B Military exercises in the use of the lance,
   facsimile of a 15th century miniature.

C Frankish fibula, jewelled gold fasteners, courtesy of The Metropolitan Museum of Art,
   gift of J. Pierpont Morgan, 1917.

D Military costumes of the 11th century, after
   Bayeux tapestries.

E Wild men and Moors, detail of a South
   German tapestry of the 14th-15th centuries,
   courtesy of Museum of Fine Arts, Boston, the
   Charles Potter Kling Fund.

F The raising up of a Frankish lord.

F

IX
Alas, the Iron!

IT so happened that King Desiderius of the Lombards and his Dukes incurred the wrath both of the Pope and of Charles, leader of the Franks. Desiderius was confident of his safety because Charles and the Pope did not get along very well. When he heard that Charles was leading an army south to chastise the Lombards for their seizure of papal property, he was quite surprised. But he was not alarmed. His capital city of Pavia was blessed with great fortifications. He had no doubt that he could outlast any siege which Charles could put upon his city. Strategically located at the entrance of the fertile valley of the River Po, Pavia would protect Lombardy from the ravages of the Franks.

On the night before the arrival of the Frankish Army, the King met with his captain of the guard on the parapets above the city. They marched around, filled with great satisfaction. It was a most cozy prospect, like a ship, high above the green fields and the rushing river.

"We shall be snug here, and outlast the rash Franks."

King Desiderius had great confidence in his soldiery who were schooled in daring attacks from out of their castled towns, wreaking havoc on besieging armies and returning to safety behind the thick walls. The city's granaries were bulging. Great stocks of food had been laid in and secret tunneled accesses would provide more if need be. The river itself would provide sustenance, for the rushing Po was not to be fettered by friend or foe.

And so Desiderius went to sleep feeling quite secure. He had left word to be called shortly after dawn, and was not prepared for the frenzied scuffle which occurred outside his bedchamber in the darkness of night.

"Wake the King!"

"But his orders!"

The King emerged and quieted his courtiers. The Captain of the Guard bowed and informed him that he had seen moonlight glinting madly all through the valley around the castle, as if the river had overflowed its banks. Of course, a flood would be to their advantage. Charles and his armies could not besiege them if the plain had flooded. But at this time of year? On a clear and cloudless night? The King commanded his courtiers to dress and meet him on the parapets.

The King's party mounted the stone steps in silence. Desiderius stepped up onto the ramparts in the last darkness of night. He gave the password to the sentry who saluted smartly. The moon reflected off the familiar river; it illuminated the familiar rows of poplar down the great alleys of the formal garden; it glinted off the distant mountains. And just as the Captain of the Guard had reported, random reflections of the moon appeared throughout the entire plain, as far as the eye could see. Indeed, it looked as if the river had overflowed its banks, flooding the entire valley. However, there was something odd about these new reflections. They danced about, disappeared, rose and fell, as if the moon were reflecting off of a choppy sea.

As the king and his party peered out into the countryside, the moon dipped below the further hills. The sky began to lighten. The King strolled along the parapet, feeling distinctly uneasy. His stomach heaved with nausea. He paused and peered down into the darkness below. A dawn breeze rose and the trees began to sway. Ordinarily this was the moment of the dawn bird-flighting, a favorite event for the King who liked to think that his kingdom was comprised not only of so many villages, farms, castles and people, but also of the beasts of the forests and the birds of the air. The birds he much preferred to all his other subjects. But this morning the birds were silent. He wondered if the flood had driven them off—if, indeed, it was a flood down there in the gloom of the valley floor.

Now the sun began to rise. The King was pleased that his mountains rose to the north, to the west, and to the south of his capital, but not to the east, where the great broad plain descended gently towards the sea. Nothing impeded the very first rays of the morning sun from reaching his castle. He moved to the eastern parapet, one small king about to receive that first sight of the great king of the earth. The orange arc humped up and as a warm ray reached the King's brow, he heard a cry. His Captain and the rest of the guard stared with awe down on the valley. He looked down now too, and saw, illumined by the rising sun, the armies of Charles Magnus, King of the Franks, surrounding his castle, filling the countryside, massed and glittering in the morning sunlight. It appeared to King Desiderius that all the horses of the world had been gathered for this mighty show, and on their backs, the armor-clad knights of the north. It looked as if the earth had heaved up its veiny bowels, substituting the magnificent metal of its interior for the soft green growing plants of its surface.

Wherever the King looked, sun glanced off iron, shattering into glittering fragments which dazzled his eyes. A great iron sea had flooded his kingdom, offering him no quarter. No wonder the birds had fled. He fell fainting to the stones, and was heard to murmur:

"Alas, the iron!"

A

B

C

D

E

A A Carolingian castle from a 9th century
manuscript.

B Siege of Toulouse, 1218, bas relief in Church
of St. Nazaire, Carcassonne.

C Goblet, said to be Charlemagne's.

D Coin of Charlemagne, King of the Franks.

E Arms and armor, 16th century France, courtesy of The Metropolitan Museum of Art,
Rogers Fund, and gift of William H. Riggs,
1917.

F Portrait of Charlemagne.

G Image from sword of Charlemagne.

G

X

Three Friends and a Militant Order

IN the Cistercian monastery called St. Wulaf on the banks of the River Grete, three close friends, Rothkav, Egbert, and Wendilo, received permission from a lenient prior to meet in the scriptorium before dawn three times a week in order to hold debate on the Holy Scripture. Such a morning meeting was an unusual dispensation among the Cistercians. Although personal relationships inevitably grew up among the brothers, the order did not welcome them. In this militant organization, work and devotion were the twin occupations within which a living salvation was to be discovered. All else was distraction.

For centuries, monastic religious orders had been busy creating a new empire on earth—an empire created not by military conquest, but by orderly disciplined work based on a mechanical concept of time. The hours of the day were ordered according to the seven periods of devotion; intense labor filled the intervals. The battle was long and difficult: no less a struggle to conquer the wilderness of nature than to conquer the wilderness of the spirit which threatened the Western world after the fall of Rome. The friendly conversation of Rothkav, Egbert, and Wendilo, even upon holy subjects, could find no justification within such a system. Even more unusual was the fact that one of the three friends, Wendilo, had been allowed to give up the habit. Wendilo had become a lay brother, one of a devout troop who helped run the monastery but were not bound strictly to the rule of the order. Relationships between monks and the lay brothers were discouraged.

And yet no one at St. Wulaf's begrudged Rothkav, Egbert and Wendilo their dispensation to meet and share this earthly trial in the cold clear early morning hours. The three had been part of the founding mission of the monastery. They had labored on the very walls of the abbey, and each, in his way, enjoyed particularly high status within the order. Rothkav's scholarship, illuminations, and commentary surpassed any in Christendom. Egbert was a great and kindly teacher whose pupils had become respected teachers wherever they went. He taught the love of harsh discipline, for, as he said, only through the observance of strict limits to the flesh could the spirit vault towards the grandeur of God. Wendilo, an excellent sculptor, was the technical genius of St. Wulaf's. He had been the original pioneer who had ventured out into the wilderness and had chosen this very site on which to build a monastery. With supple limbs and a clear voice with which to sing his helpers on, Wendilo had provided the monastery with a mill, a smithy, and implements without compare among all the houses of the order.

One day a new abbot, William, arrived to take the burden of the abbey on his shoulders. William was no stranger to Egbert, Rothkav, and Wendilo. He had grown up in the same village and had taken his novitiate with them. He was neither as devout as Rothkav, nor as scholarly as Egbert, nor as graceful or adept as Wendilo, and he had always felt excluded from their friendship. Abbot William looked upon the early morning meeting of the three friends with particular disfavor, and yet he dared not make an issue of the matter. In order to entrap the three, he employed a newly ordained monk, Scrofold, as his spy.

Shortly after the arrival of Abbot William, Wendilo came to the early morning meeting in the scriptorium trembling over a passionate dream from which he had just wakened. This dream had first come to him, like a vision, upon his solitary mission into the wilderness to locate a proper site for St. Wulaf's, years ago. On the very night that he had discovered the stately oak forest on the banks of the River Grete, the verdant meadows and the powerful stream which now turned their mill, he had fallen asleep, praying for a sign from the Lord to confirm his discovery. The dream which he experienced that night had returned again and again to haunt him. This morning he could no longer keep his torment a secret.

Wendilo dreamed that he died and crossed a narrow footbridge over a frothing river. Arriving upon the luminous banks of Paradise, he strode forward joyfully. Friendly beasts rubbed against his legs; all manner of comely men and women greeted him with welcoming smiles and embraces. And yet doubt and fear grew within him. Without knowing why, he began to search. His anxiety increased. Wherever he looked he saw nobles and peasants and monks of every order, but nowhere did he see anyone attired in the dress of the Cistercians. Where were his beloved friends Rothkav and Egbert? How could it be that he, Wendilo, the most unworthy of the three, should have been admitted to this place before them? He asked after Egbert and Rothkav everywhere, but no one knew of them. Finally he reached a meadow by the side of a river where a stream lined with oaks entered. It was an exact replica of a site he had seen somewhere before. He threw himself upon the ground and began to weep for his lost brethren.

To his surprise, the ground beneath him rose, alive and warm. He felt himself lifted up. Opening his eyes, he found himself cradled in the arms of a beautiful lady. It was Mary herself, Mother of God, radiant in green flowing garments, laced with ribbons as blue and silvery as the streams and rivers of the land. Her gentle voice inquired of his tears.

"How is it, most Holy Lady," he replied, that I see none of our order in this place? Wherefore are the servants Egbert and Rothkav, who honor you so devoutly, shut out from so blessed a company?"

Seeing his trouble, the Queen of Heaven answered, "Do not reproach me thus, O sad young monk. Those of your order are so beloved and familiar to me that I cherish them even next to my own body, especially your two close friends." She threw open her cloak, revealing the body of a healthy young woman with soft round breasts. A sweet odor rose up from her like a meadow after rain. There at home on the sweet and glowing flesh of the Lady of the Lord, Wendilo saw his two friends, along with the innumerable multitude of his own order. Monks, lay brothers, and nuns stood between her breasts, they were sheltered in her armpits and cradled in the soft hair of her crotch. Wendilo reached out his arms and found himself welcomed by Rothkav and Egbert. As he clasped them, the body of Mary lay down beneath him once more. A multitude of voices rose in prayer, and that sweet odor grew richer and richer, merging with the scent of a fertilized field, of wet hay, of ripening apples. All around him now the monks, lay brothers, and nuns toiled, groaning, digging, hauling, praying, and soon out of the rich land rose the spire of a newly built monastery. A water-wheel turned in the frothing stream. Bells chimed. Work stopped; prayers rose; work started; bells chimed again; and his brethren labored while he found himself lying upon the body of Our Lady who had become earth. His hands, grasping flesh, brought up black loam, the fertile soil of river bottoms. Slowly he felt himself drawn into the wondrous body. Slowly the rich warm muck embraced him, and he awoke in an ecstasy of terror.

After a long silence, Rothkav expelled a small sigh, assuring Wendilo that the beautiful body of nature which Wendilo had caressed with such extravagance had been but the soul of the world; the flowering of earth stood for the true promise of salvation. Egbert objected, with a kindly, ironic smile. Unquestionably, he insisted, Wendilo, like any man, was being tormented by normal sexual desire, but in life he had not yielded to the temptations of flesh. Just as in the dream, so in life, their handsome friend had chosen God's earth as a road to salvation. Wendilo, Egbert concluded, had bent all his considerable talents to the cultivation of earth for the benefit of the saving order of the Cistercians. For Rothkav, nature existed merely as God's metaphor, a book of gloriously illuminated images through which man could glimpse divine salvation. In Egbert's opinion, the world was much more than a metaphor. It was God's creation, and an observant rational man could discover God in the workings of nature just as surely as he could meet Him through faith and prayer.

Poor Wendilo leaned one way and then another. For him nature was sometimes a mother who yielded up her riches freely, and at other times a capricious woman who had to be seduced for her benefices. He could hardly speak of God's role in the matter without blushing. Happy by day in the glory of natural beauty and the cleverness of his hands, Wendilo was tortured at night.

Just as his friends finished discussing his dream, Wendilo caught the sound of a gasp outside the window, and the slight rasp of cloth against stone. Without a change in tone or inflection, he answered Egbert's argument in Latin, warning his friends that an eavesdropper lurked outside the window. There was no doubt in his mind that they would find Scrofold, the tattler, Abbot William's spy, listening to their discussion. Scrofold's crude grasp of Latin was a joke of the monastery. For this reason, Wendilo continued in that language.

"The scoundrel has delivered himself into our hands. Rothkav, go into the church and begin to pray. Egbert, my great disciplinarian, seize the scourge hanging in the hallway and slip outside to the window where you will find a likely subject for your stout arm."

Whispering a short prayer for them all, Rothkav crept off into the chapel. A delighted Egbert slipped through the hallway. Hefting the scourge from one hand to another, he sidled along the wall towards the window where he made out a form huddled against the wall. At that moment the window burst open and the huge hand of Wendilo descended, grasping the eavesdropper by the hair and lifting him off his feet. Now, grinning widely, Egbert set to with his scourge, hailing blows over the body of the defenseless creature who began to cry piteously for help.

"I've caught the Devil, I've caught the Devil," Wendilo shouted. Egbert stole away.

Out of the buildings rushed the brethren, bearing lanterns. The light revealed the figure of Scrofold, hanging listlessly in the grasp of Wendilo, like a fresh-caught fish, twitching slightly.

"It's Scrofold, the abbot's familiar."

"Let him down! It's Scrofold."

Still Wendilo held his victim, turning him half around in the air and scrutinizing him carefully. "It looks like Scrofold," he said, "but the Devil can take many forms. Be careful!" He let the terrified monk drop.

"I've been beaten, I've been beaten," Scrofold moaned.

Minding Wendilo's warning, the other monks kept their distance. "But who beat you? Who beat him, Wendilo?" they asked.

"It must have been the Lord's Angel," replied Wendilo.

∴

For two days Scrofold hid himself away, knowing that the abbot would miss him. Then he let himself be found. After politely inquiring about Scrofold's health, the abbot proceeded to question him about what he had overheard at the window of the scriptorium.

"And what do they say about the Scriptures?"

"The Scriptures?" Scrofold replied. And he reported that the text which the three friends had discussed the morning of his beating had not been the text of the Holy Scriptures, but a dream of Wendilo in which he had intercourse with the naked body of the Virgin.

"And the others?" asked the Abbot, shaking himself and standing abruptly. "Did they chastise him for such unseemly thoughts?"

"Quite the contrary," continued the spying monk. "They assured him that such dreams were quite normal. They admitted that they too dreamt of carnal relations and told him that his purity of soul was proven by the fact that the woman he had chosen was none other than the Virgin Mother."

"Blasphemy." The abbot stared at the carving of the Pieta across the room for some time, his fingers drumming slowly upon the table. When he began to speak, his words came resonantly to his lips as if he were addressing a congregation. "We Cistercians live at an unusual time, very much like that of Rome's glory, when whole cities arose in an instant in the midst of the wilderness. Christianity has organized itself and is ready to leap. To us has been given the task of taking the first step in a glorious conquest. Mankind will surely spread to the ends of the earth. The question remains: Who will lead them, the sacred or the profane? I see great cities of priests, dedicated to God and the Virgin Mother, cultivating earth and fulfilling its development. We owe it to God to lay out these exemplary cities, for otherwise the Devil will take possession of the earth as he has in times past.

"Order! Regularity! Rule! These must be our mottos in the battle. Exceptions cannot be allowed."

∴

Several days later, Scrofold came to Abbot William with a plan. "St. Wulaf's has reached its maturity," he explained. "It is time we become mother house to a great brood of new outposts in the eastern wilderness. Certain older monks with great talent and experience could be sent along. If you were to send your three burdens off, one at a time . . ."

"Ah, Scrofold," exclaimed the Abbot, "you shall become clerk of works, charged with the conquest of the eastern regions."

"Then Egbert should lead the way," said Scrofold. "He is the strongest willed of the three. He will be like a great lantern to light the way to the inexperienced pioneers."

Joyously Abbot William sent for Egbert to inform him of his privilege. The abbot had to send several times for the great teacher. Egbert rarely left his schoolrooms, not even to attend services and mass, saying that it was better to teach others to sing than to sing himself. Nor did he attend the chapter house, where faults were confessed and discipline inflicted. His excuse in this was that he had to reprove others and punish them all day long. Abbot William, only too aware of Egbert's omissions, insisted today that the teacher attend him. Finally, Egbert came. When the abbot announced that Egbert had been chosen to accompany the new mission into the eastern wilderness, he did so with a wide smile: "It is a great honor we bestow on you, to carry God's word and his rule out among the heathen." He gazed eagerly at the clever narrow face before him.

"I have already had the honor once," replied Egbert, grasping the back of a nearby chair to still his trembling.

"Nevertheless, you shall have it again." The good abbot stared down at the white knuckles clutching the chair. "You deserve as much."

"But I am no longer fit to travel. And what of my books?"

"You need but one book to teach the word of God."

"My feet?" Egbert moved about so little he had come to have great trouble with his feet. Much of the day he kept his feet encased in soft slippers, high upon a foot-stool as he taught. He scarcely wore out a pair of shoes once every two years.

"We shall provide you with many pairs of new stout shoes."

The prospect made Egbert feel faint. "But I have lost the . . . the habit of motion."

"The habit of motion?"

Egbert smiled grimly. He could see that his protests would do him no good. He would have to suffer the rude jostles of markets and towns, the rough stones of roads, freezing nights, wild beasts, savages, wind and rain, all for the glory of God and the Cistercian order.

"Thank you, Brother," he bowed, "thank you for the great honor."

Scrofold was not one to let the occasion pass by without the proper ceremony. Day after day he visited Egbert's schoolroom, inquiring solicitously how he could help the teacher prepare himself. He insisted upon measuring Egbert's feet and supervised the making of a half-dozen pair of shoes, which he had Egbert try out in the fields. At last, poor Egbert fell ill from his extreme anxiety and from the walks out in the cold muddy fields with his new shoes. He took to his bed.

Without permission, neglecting their duties, Rothkav and Wendilo came to his cell to attend him. No one dared disturb them. In the small enclosed space with white walls, Wendilo and Rothkav propped up their dear friend seven times a day to join them in devotions. Otherwise, not a word was spoken. The light of day brightened the thick window embrasure three times. As the dusk of the third day darkened the cell, Egbert gave a feverish hand to each of his friends. With his last energy, he attempted to pass on to them the strength of his love, the endurance of his emotion. He would never have to leave the sanctuary the three of them had built upon the banks of the River Grete.

Under guise of kindness, the Abbot asked Rothkav to deliver the graveside oration. When the entire monastery had been assembled at Egbert's grave, Rothkav stepped forward, took a deep breath, and clearly enunciated one sentence:

"In the midst of life, we are in death."

A wail from Wendilo greeted this speech. Rothkav hurried to comfort him. The entire assembly returned to their daily tasks with ladened hearts, thinking of the living death within which they prepared for eternal salvation.

Wendilo was given very little time to grieve for his friend. Instead of sending him off to the wilderness, which he might find too congenial, Scrofold arranged for the abbot to lend the excellent sculptor to the mayor of a nearby city to carve a statue of the Virgin Mary which would grace the square of the church of that thriving place. Scrofold suspected that Wendilo would find the temptations of the city a torment past enduring.

As soon as he arrived in the city, Wendilo requested that a tent be erected around the uncarved block, and that he be allowed to work undisturbed. Wendilo himself pegged down every foot of the tent. He asked that food be brought to the flap twice a day.

Week after week the hammer and chisel could be heard, accompanied by beautiful song. Every few hours the famous Cistercian lay brother stopped to pray. As time went on, the sound of the chisel grew more insistent. A request for candles was found on one evening's empty tray. Work went on now through the whole night without a moment's pause for prayer. During this stage of the task the songs which accompanied the chisel lost their heavenly quality. A poignant tone pervaded them, and they echoed certain primitive airs no longer heard in the vicinity of the city. They were songs in an ancient dialect. Some maintained that the words told of happenings and desires unfit for the mouth or mind of a holy man. And then, one day, the sound of the chisel and of the gorgeous voice were both still.

Fearing illness or accident, the mayor himself appeared. He cut open the tent flap and intrepidly entered. There was no sound. Outside, the entire town gathered. The mayor reappeared in a few minutes, his face red, his eyes rolling. He seemed in a daze. The crowd rushed past him, into the tent. The sound of shocked amazement came from inside. Others pushed in, until the tent fell. When the debris had been cleared away and the police had moved everyone away from the site, Wendilo's sculpture could at last be clearly seen. There, lying on her back, was a heavy-breasted, deep-thighed, sensual woman. Every detail of the female anatomy had been realistically rendered. The identity of the statue was indisputable: the crown of Mary graced her brow. The clear beautiful features of the Virgin Mother stared skyward in ecstasy.

That very day, the town militia destroyed the statue. Wendilo was not heard of again.

Meanwhile, Rothkav devoted himself to illuminating a copy of the canonical epistles in Greek. His art was fired by the passion of his mourning. Never had any of his brother monks ever seen such beautiful illumination. It would be, in their estimation, the crowning achievement of their age. In four years, Rothkav was almost three-quarters done. Visitors began to appear from beyond the sea to study the work in progress. Rothkav kept his manuscript carefully stored in a bin, high upon the upper shelves of the library. One day, supervising the restoration of one wall of the library, quite by chance, Scrofold came upon the beautifully wrought volume. In a moment, without thinking, he removed the exquisite pages, and carried them to his rooms where he proceeded to mutilate them, both with knife and pen. Within the hour, he returned the pages to their hiding place. As Rothkav did not look back over his work very often, it was some months before he removed the bin to discover the destruction of his great art.

He spoke of his discovery to no one. He did not for a moment wonder who had been the human agent of this devastating blow. He knew that ultimately it was the hand of the Lord, a punishment for his excessive love of his work, and his excessive mourning after his lost friends. From that day on, Rothkav's eyes grew dimmer. Within a year, he was completely blind. Nor did he die mercifully after this, but he lived on for many years in complete silence and darkness, praying to the Lord for forgiveness. In his final moments, he confessed that his faith had not yet overcome his sadness at the loss of his two friends. The attending priest closed his eyes, sure that Rothkav would be damned.

∵

As for Scrofold, he did not escape unharmed. Ever since his beating at the hands of the friends, the clerk of works had brooded at his lack of learning, and, in particular, at his fuzzy knowledge of Latin. He begged, and received from the abbot, private instruction. Soon he became so enamored with learning that he began to neglect his duties. He spent his days wandering about his rooms, murmuring the glorious Latin words and phrases he had learned. At services, he found himself mimicking the benedictions of the abbot, and, late at night, he practised giving the service exactly as the abbot gave it. When the bishop visited, Scrofold followed him about from morning to evening, until the bishop asked him to be removed from his sight. And then one day Scrofold was found missing from the abbey. At the same time, someone broke into the bishop's rooms and stole his most precious ceremonial robes and goblets.

Some weeks later, on one of the great roads leading to Italy, it was reported that a grand bishop of the church was proceeding on a personal pilgrimage to Rome. At every stop he received petitioners, gave out blessings, and conducted services. As he proceeded, his company grew, all of his attendants wearing the robes of the Cistercian order. Along the route, following the passage of this grand seigneur of the church, came reports of thefts of church property, silver and gold, robes and costumes, and relics of all sorts. Shortly before he reached the border of Italy the imposter was captured and unmasked by the king's men. It was Scrofold, clerk of works of St.Wulaf's Abbey. After a quick trial held before the order could intervene, Scrofold was hung without ceremony as a common thief.

∵

Unmarked by sadness or disappointment, Abbot William rose high in the Cistercian movement. He never looked back, nor was his sleep disturbed by dreams, nor his waking thoughts by memories of those who had perished in his wake. He lived certain that he had done nothing but good works during his entire life. Unfortunately, Satan's victory in the world poisoned his old age. The Cistercian movement, like all those before, slowly waned. Secular cities multiplied and grew out of the very seeds planted by the brave pioneers of that militant order.

A

B

C

D

E

A   Presentation of St. Bernard, founder of the Cistercian Order, by his parents. Flemish stained-glass, 16th century, courtesy of The Metropolitan Museum of Art, bequest of George D. Pratt, 1941.

B   St. Bernard with the monks of Citeaux takes possession of the Abbey of Clairvaux, from a 15th century manuscript.

C   Agriculture in the 11th century (Ms. Cott. Claud. B. IV.).

D   Feeding chickens, 14th century (Loutrell Psalter).

E   Illuminated letter S, Virgin and Child, early 15th century, Verona, Italy, courtesy of The Metropolitan Museum of Art, Rogers Fund, 1912.

F   Agriculture in the 11th century (Ms. Harl. 603).

F

The
Hoop of
Thorns

XI

A Plague of Life

SOMEWHERE in the cold vastness of
Central Asia in the distant past, a small rod-like creature appeared:
Bacillus pestis, a specialized member of an immense group of one-celled
creatures called bacteria which inhabited the entire globe. Two hundred
and fifty thousand of these bacilli would fit into a single grain of dirt,
but each one was an independent unit of life, each with a remarkable
coding compound which insured that the offspring would almost exactly duplicate the parent.

Bacillus pestis made its home within the bloodstream of various wild
squirrel-like rodents. There, given the proper shelter, temperature and
nourishment, it grew, procreated simply by dividing in half, and multiplied. Unfortunately, as *Bacillus pestis* grew, it discharged waste products
which injured the tissue of its host animal, eventually killing it. Once the
host died, *Bacillus pestis*, without legs or wings, should have perished
also, except that it had already found a mode of transportation to another
living host. In the course of its evolution, the bacteria was fortunate
enough to encounter a small compact wingless flea which had made its
way eastward from the Nile valley. This flea lived solely upon the blood
of warm-blooded animals, among them the very rodents which provided housing for *Bacillus pestis*.

The Egyptian flea was admirably constructed for the task of trans-
porting bacteria from one host to another. The flea's flat sides allowed
it to slide easily through the hairs of the host animal; its backward

pointed spines assisted it in resisting the efforts of the host to scratch it off; and its long hind legs gave it remarkable powers of leaping, fifty to one hundred times the length of its body, so that it easily could move from one rodent to another. With its penetrating beak, the flea would make an incision in the infected rodent's skin, sucking in the nourishing blood along with some five thousand bacilli which would then multiply in the flea's stomach and throat. Within a few days the throat of the flea would become so clogged with the multiplying jellied masses of *Bacillus pestis* that blood could no longer pass down into the stomach. Thus, when the flea made its incision upon a new host and began to suck, its throat, full of bacilli, would bulge out. As soon as the flea stopped sucking, the walls of its throat would recoil, forcing blood and bacilli back into the incision where *Bacillus pestis* could flourish.

The rodent provided an ideal habitat for the growth of the bacteria. In return, *Bacillus pestis* provided the rodent population with an important service: weeding out the old, the sick and the weak from the rodent ranks so that more of the resources—food and shelter—were available for the healthy. Healthy rodents developed an immunity to the bacteria, thus ensuring a continuing population within which *Bacillus pestis*, aided by its flea carrier, could search out likely candidates. Even the flea found a happy living situation in this complicated arrangement. The large communal burrows of the rodents proved ideal nurseries in which to raise flea larvae. In this way, nature created a happy balance between bacteria, flea, and rodent.

During the last years of the thirteenth and the early years of the fourteenth centuries, the happy arrangement between *Bacillus pestis*, the Asiatic rodent, and the flea from the Nile was disrupted by a climate change. The planet earth wobbled in orbit; the sun sent up unusual flares which triggered vast fields of energy coursing through the solar system; the hot molten core of earth released explosive gases through fissures in the crust. The weather became unpredictable. Glaciers advanced. Unusually cold winters were followed by floods which were then followed by parching droughts. Throughout the planet, destructive famines came after years of plenty. During the good years, the rodent population multiplied as it never had before. Litter followed litter, burrows were filled to bursting. The plains and mountains of Transbailakia, Mongolia, Manchuria, Siberia, and Russian Turkestan abounded in basking, gamboling tarabagans; susliks thrived in southeastern Russia, and gerbils multiplied in Iranian Turkestan and Transcaspia. The Egyptian flea thrived also, as did *Bacillus pestis* in a modest manner. However, when lean years followed the fat ones, the land could no longer provide for the vastly increased rodent population. Large rodent migrations took place across the Asiatic plains towards the West. At this time, in the midst of general famine, *Bacillus pestis* found its own feast. The hungry, weak, and driven population of migrating rodents provided ideal hosts for the bacteria. *Bacillus pestis* itself now grew into a vast hungry population, choking its carrier fleas, driving them out of hunger to seek new warm bodies as the wild rodents died in droves. It was like a troop of mountain nomads sweeping from east to west in search of living space for their hungry stomachs; it was, in fact, an immense wave of living creatures, consuming, growing and destroying in order to survive. Soon the flea was multiplying more quickly than its host, and the bacteria much more quickly than both together.

∵

While *Bacillus pestis* remained pretty much confined to Central Asia for thousands of years, a completely different species of life, *Homo sapiens*, evolved its own unique method of survival and spread over much of the earth. This two-legged, thinly haired animal had learned to survive through group living, the use of tools, and complicated communications systems. As time went on, *Homo sapiens* proved to be a fairly successful life form, its population rising gradually. Then, with the discovery of agriculture, the population spurted. Civilizations rose and fell; fields bloomed with produce destined for the human stomach; forests yielded up trees to make houses and ships; quarries yielded up stone for buildings, bridges, and roads. From time to time, the species declined. The earth became overused; wars within the species depleted resources; and the species' own ingenious political and social systems strangled its power and ingenuity. One such decline occurred in the rich lands surrounding the great warm sea called the Mediterranean. There the idea became fixed in the collective mind that all life would soon come to an end. However, with the discovery of land to the north and the use of new agricultural tools and methods, the population expanded again, colonizing the wilderness of Europe and reviving commerce and industry.

To fuel this great expansion, *Homo sapiens* harnessed nature. The water wheel, with the use of refined gearing, spread throughout northern Europe, hammering ore, grinding grain, and fulling textiles. Windmills were converted to practical uses and rose in great groves as if they were trees of the forest. Centers of trade and industry grew up. Once more *Homo sapiens* congregated in great cities. The architecture was dominated by Gothic spires soaring towards an invisible God which humans believed ruled over them. Yet, even as these temples of God were being completed, they were undermined by new ideas about human beings and nature symbolized by great mechanical clocks in the centers of the cities. At London, Canterbury, Paris, in Milan, St. Albans, Glastonbury, Avignon, and Padua, planets wheeled in cycles and epicycles, angels trumpeted, cocks crew, and apostles, kings, and prophets marched and countermarched at the booming of the hours. The public delighted at the mechanical marvels which represented progress in the use of machinery to accomplish the tasks necessary for the success of the species. A falling weight set in motion a train of geared wheels while an oscillatory escapement mechanism prevented the weight from accelerating too quickly as it fell. Humankind marked time.

There arose among the populace a conscious and general lust for natural energy to solve all human needs. The cosmos was thought of as a vast reservoir of energies to be tapped and used according to human intentions. Men thought that in a very short time the species would invent a machine which would run perpetually. One of the great priests of the age became the first to speak of the universe as a vast mechanical clock, created and set running by God so that all the wheels moved with perfect harmony. This metaphor would return to haunt the species, eventually destroying its most cherished beliefs.

Nature did not forgive human excesses lightly. *Homo sapiens*, with its ingenious mind and hands, was proving too successful, multiplying in much the same embarrassing manner as the wild rodent of Asia. When the planet wobbled, the sun sent up its flares, the earth quaked and the climate changed, mankind was no more ready to adjust than its fellow

life species. At the end of the thirteenth and the beginning of the fourteenth centuries, the intensely cold winters led to a striking advance of
polar and alpine glaciers; high rainfalls caused a rise in the sea level,
shrinking arable land; cultivation of cereals and the vine in northern
countries almost ceased, and wheat-growing areas declined. A series of
disastrous harvests and famines struck at the once thriving populations.
Prices for food rose alarmingly, and many of the human species died of
starvation. The poor began to eat dogs, cats, the leavings of doves, and
even human children. *Homo sapiens* was plagued by its own success.
There were too many people with not enough fertile land on which to
feed. While some fled, most people remained in their cities, and villages
and farms and suffered. Unlike rodents, the human species had lost the
appetite for migration. In addition to their economic woes, the very
political groupings which had aided in their success now became a terror.
Wars, both big and small, disrupted farming and commerce, destroyed
the vigorous and healthy, and further weakened the population. In
mind, body, and spirit, *Homo sapiens* in the West was thus prepared to
embrace disaster when it came on the bodies of small beasts.

In Asia, at this very moment, the starving flea found a rich new
grazing ground on the flesh of the black rat, that great companion to the
human species. *Rattus rattus* particularly loved ocean voyages, glorying
in the rich human leavings to be found in the holds of ships. It was not
long before the black rat, carrying the Egyptian flea and *Bacillus pestis*,
found its way, along with spices, silks, sugar, and jewels, to the great
ports of Mediterranean Europe. As the spices, jewels, and cloths were
hauled out of the holds of ships, so the black rats, covered with infected
fleas, crept down bow and stern lines, finding their way to the burrows
of cousins throughout the cities. Unlike the merchants, *Rattus rattus*
brought with it a living, growing import. Within the city, rats began
to die, their cells overwhelmed by the poisonous wastes of their unin-
vited visitors. Before long, in full view of the great town clock towers—
symbols of humankind's mastery of the natural world—the first flea
leaped, landed upon human skin, dipped its mandibles and labrum, made
its incision, and began to suck. Unable to move the human blood past
the thick jellied mass of bacteria which blocked its throat, the flea regur-
gitated a goodly number of *Bacillus pestis* into the wound. There, in sight

of the wheeling planets, in the proud center of which earth twirled self-importantly, two successful forms of life made each other's acquaintance.

Once more, *Bacillus pestis* had found its way into a system unable to cope with its rapid multiplication and its toxic wastes. *Homo sapiens* had not yet developed defenses against this thriving visitor. Ravaged by famines and war, the Europeans provided a perfect host for this unfamiliar life form which came to it from the Orient. Soon eyes dimmed and tongues thickened with a thin white fur. A dull stupor overcame first one, then another, and then a third citizen. Great weakness followed; burning and itching pains occurred around the neck, in armpits, and groin. On the second or third day, hard swellings arose in all three spots, swellings ranging in size from that of an almond to that of an orange, protuberances which now and then broke open to exude a disgusting pus. Temperatures rose to dangerous heights, the victim began to vomit, to complain of terrible headaches, giddiness, thirst, and an intolerance to light. His stomach, back, and limbs ached, and often he moaned and screamed before he lapsed into apathy, passing into delirium. The death was a terrible one.

Within a few years, *Bacillus pestis* spread to every major city and region in western Europe. Almost a third of the human population sickened and died. The Great Plague ravished not only the body of *Homo sapiens*, but its mind also, and its dreams worst of all. No one at the time could explain the mechanism by which this terrible sickness spread. Many hypotheses were advanced—from the contagion of evil vapors, to a heavenly conjunction of Saturn, Jupiter, and Mars. But after such explanation, the question still remained, "Why?" Even if a plodding, observant man had come forward to announce that the plague had been caused by a population of living creatures too small to be seen with the naked eye, creatures carried about by barely discernible fleas who had drunk them from the bloodstream of black rats, his wildly improbable tale might have been accepted along with the others, occasioning the same question, "Why?"

The thundering reply from the pulpits, "God's punishment!" began to seem inadequate. Doubts crept in. What about the children? Did they have to suffer so cruelly for the sins of their elders? The babies too, covered with great pus-laden swellings, thrashing about in mortal agony?

And such grand devastation? Did the Lord require so many deaths to pay for gluttony, greed, usury, lust? So shocked were the Europeans at the plague's destruction that deep within their souls most began to suspect that the plague was the work, not of divine wrath, but of another more mysterious force to whom God had resigned the world.

At the very moment when human skins were being penetrated by the beaks of infected fleas, eternity was ceasing to serve as a measure and focus for human actions. Even before their eyes glazed over and their tongues thickened with disease, human beings were beginning to worship not the soaring steeple of God, but the clock beneath, which was producing the greatest standard products man was ever to make: hours, minutes, and seconds. Slowly a belief in a world of mathematically measurable sequences was taking root, a world in which man's power and judgment proved to be the final arbiter—a special world which later would be called by scientists the only true world. Once God had shown his indifference, or his impotence, human beings would look only to the clock and beneath it to synchronize their actions and to measure their mortality.

And yet the worship of science and human industry which eventually replaced the love of God and the fear of the devil proved no more satisfactory to *Homo sapiens*. In time, the species learned to protect itself from the ravages of *Bacillus pestis*. Suffering and death remained, and the question "Why?" still echoed through its dreams.

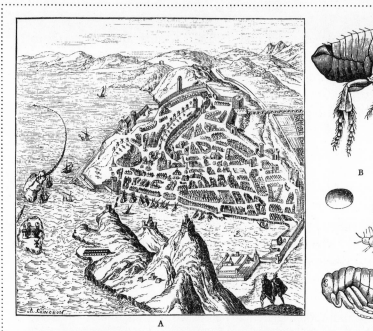

A

B

C

D

E

F

le charretier

la vieille

l'abbesse

le triomphe

l'empereur

l'astrologien

l'usurier.

Le juge

le médecin

G

A View and plan of the port of Marseille in the 16th century.

B Development of a flea.

C Colony of marmots.

D St. Gregory institutes the Litanies during the plague from The Belles Heures by Jean, Duke of Berry, French, 15th century, courtesy of The Metropolitan Museum of Art, The Cloisters Collection, purchase, 1954.

E The Office of the Dead from The Belles Heures of Jean, Duke of Berry, courtesy of The Metropolitan Museum of Art, The Cloisters Collection, purchase, 1954.

F St. Martin and the Beggar, Flemish-Brabant, about 1500, courtesy of The Philadelphia Museum of Art, The George Grey Barnard Collection.

G The Dance of the Dead, facsimile of wood engravings after the work of Holbein, 16th century.

H University Chancellor in a costume to frighten off the plague.

H

XII

Tearless Before
the Maker

ONE hot August morning, a closed carriage pulled up on a side street of Gottwald, a small market town in southern Germany. Three policemen descended, followed by the town provost, who proceeded to knock discreetly upon the back door of a respectable house. Instantly the door opened. The four visitors were hurried into a cool kitchen where the policemen were offered coffee and chairs. The host, vicar of the local church, ushered the provost into the main hall, in the middle of which stood a large linen chest blocking the way. The vicar's wife stepped around the awkwardly placed chest, greeted the provost warmly, and offered him tea in the drawing-room. The lady then went to call her mother, who was the object of the provost's visit.

"You understand," said the provost, sipping his tea rather noisily, "that if your mother-in-law had remained in Linz . . ."

"I understand completely," said the Vicar, his eyes raised to the ceiling, "and I've been very grateful for your . . . forbearance."

"In fact, I've done my best not to pursue this matter. Your brother-in-law's libel suit, however . . ."

"My brother-in-law is another story completely, with his petitions and law-suits, his treatises and theories—it's a wonder anything gets done in this world. Imagine appointing a man to the Imperial Court who has declared, in print, that God made geometry before he made the world!"

"But then the emperor who appointed him was mad himself."

"And why should the Court be interested in the stars? Conjunctions and disjunctions—whether the sun goes around the earth or vice versa. I'm content to know it rises and sets every day."

"Where it's supposed to, just as God made it."

"Indeed," the vicar nodded profoundly, happy to be making a good impression on his visitor.

"Your brother-in-law makes predictions too?"

"So they say."

"And he's been excommunicated?"

"Not exactly. He tends to be argumentative."

"Calvinist?"

"Just a tincture. In any case he remains in office—please remember—and within the church."

The vicar was ready to wash his hands of the whole affair. He blamed both his mother-in-law and his brother-in-law for the predicament which threatened them all. If the old lady had been less of a bad-tempered, sharp-tongued shrew, she wouldn't have the whole town howling at her heels. As for his "grand" brother-in-law, the less said the better. For all the vicar knew, Christian was the real witch of the family—if not that, then an insidious heretic and a madman.

Rousing himself, the vicar pulled the bell to ask for more tea and cakes. The provost seemed willing to empty another plate of sweets before he continued his day. A desultory conversation ensued about the evil times into which they had slid—the continuous battles between Catholic and Protestant, the terrible deprivation and violence of the wars which descended so frequently upon them, the plague which came and went at God's will—or the Devil's—and the constant threat of Satanic heresies which ringed round decent respectable citizens like themselves. Cults, frenzies, potions, humans trying to outreach God himself. The two men nodded wisely at one another. Neither admitted that they seldom thought about God these days. In fact, both believed that the August Presence had abandoned the earth to his rebellious angel, Satan, who ruled nature and disrupted the reasonable order which these two officials attempted to maintain.

The ladies finally appeared at the top of the stairs. The old woman was quite dressed up, as if she were going to a fair. As they descended, her daughter urged her to leave her valuables at home. She shook her head obstinately. She was tiny, her brown skin gnarled and weathered. Her small green eyes glinted maliciously as she minced her way down, showing off for the two gentlemen who stood in the archway to the sitting-room.

"What a surprise!" she exclaimed. "The provost himself? How considerate!" She danced up to the official and offered her hand, but when he reached for it, she drew it away with a small laugh, skipping backward like a shy young maid. "No kisses now, no touches. Who knows what might happen?"

"Mother!" the vicar and his wife said simultaneously, exhaling. Anxiously they looked towards their guest.

The provost shrugged and smiled. "Don't worry. She's obviously upset."

"Would you care for a drink of water, kind provost? My tin cup is in the kitchen." The old lady laughed and began to retreat towards the kitchen.

The vicar's wife shrieked and covered her mouth—for it was charged that various burghers of Gottwald had become violently ill after drinking water from her mother's tin cup. The wife of Sebastian Fried had died of it, so they said, and the schoolmaster Beutelsprenger had immediately fallen into a permanent paralysis. Many other charges, of course, had been laid up against Katherine Kunst: that she had cast an evil eye upon the seven children of the tailor, Hickel Schmidt, each of whom promptly fell into convulsions; that she had entered various houses through keyholes of locked doors; that she had ridden one of farmer Spittelmeister's calves to death in order to cut off a cutlet for her crazy son Joachim, the late, epileptic vagrant.

"This has gone far enough," said the vicar grimly, as he stepped between his mother-in-law and the kitchen door. "Margot!"

The vicar's wife opened the linen chest which stood in the middle of the hall. The inside was carefully made up like a bed, with two fluffed pillows and a number of down-filled comforters. "Come, Mama, let's get it over with before you make things worse than they are."

The old lady stepped nimbly under her son-in-law's grasp and danced around to the other side of the hall, gazing with delight down into the

[175]

chest. "Oh, look how comfortably they provide for their rich old Ma. My coffin will never be so handsome, I'll wager."

Margot began to cry, and her husband took her into his arms. "See what you've done!" he said sternly to the old lady.

"What I've done? But I've done nothing. I didn't accuse myself of absurd crimes, nor did I march into my house with a band of men to lay hold of me, nor did I pile a bunch of pillows into a chest and ask myself to step inside as if I were already dead."

"It was to spare you embarrassment," said her daughter.

"Spare me? That's a laugh."

"It is to your interest not to have your situation shown so openly to all your neighbors and friends.

The provost looked appealingly over the head of his sobbing wife, and the vicar nodded in agreement. The provost then stepped to the kitchen door, calling to his men, who trooped into the front hall. At this moment the front knocker sounded. Without thinking, the vicar threw the door open, and the short dark figure of his brother-in-law, Christian Kunst, burst into the hall.

"I came as soon as I got your message," said Christian to the vicar. He stepped forward to embrace his mother. The old lady accepted her son's hug reluctantly, pulling her cheek away so that his kiss landed short. He shrugged and demanded to know why the police had been summoned.

Briefly the vicar explained and then appealed for Christian's help in getting the old lady into the chest.

"Nonsense!" exclaimed Christian. "There's no need for your absurd chest, nor for an escort. My mother and I are capable of reporting to the town gate at whatever time you desire."

"That is no longer possible," said the provost. "Either we take your mother in the chest out the back door, quietly, or we shall escort her through the streets in plain view."

"The chest it shall be!" shouted Katherine gleefully. Before her son could object, she jumped over the side of the chest, landing in a sitting position in the soft interior. "Like an Indian Princess, I shall go! Carried in state."

"Mother!" said Christian, "Get out of that ridiculous chest."

"We've cut holes for air," said Margot, pointing them out to her brother, who brushed her aside.

"Then I shall be able to see all my friends," said the old lady, peering through the air holes. "I'll know who's laughing and who's crying."

The provost nodded. Two of the policemen began to lower the lid carefully, but the old lady would not lie down. Instead she grinned spitefully at her son, Christian, as if daring him to pull her from her throne.

"It won't close unless she lies down," explained one of the policemen.

As Christian lunged for his mother, she fell back to avoid his grasp. The men closed the lid down rapidly.

"Good-by my loved ones, good-by," her voice sounded hollowly out through the air holes. "They say they'll ship me to America in return for tobacco. There I shall be free from my bothersome children."

Outside, unfortunately, a hitch occurred in the proceedings. The chest would not fit through the carriage door, and no one had thought to bring a rope to lash it to the roof. Wishing to avoid any further interference from Christian, who was descending the back steps, the provost bade his men carry the chest on foot to the keep at the town gate. He leaped into the carriage, which moved swiftly off through the gathering crowd.

The chest rose and commenced its voyage on the swaying shoulders of the four policemen. Through the air holes the old lady could see the tops of heads, a face or two, the sky, a piece of her son-in-law's church, the spout of a fountain. She could hear Christian's officious voice directing the policemen to be careful with their burden. She wished he had stayed in Austria. He had always annoyed her, even when he was a child. In jail, at least she would not have to listen to his talk.

She might have subsided into her comfortable vessel had she not at that moment recognized the bonnet of her enemy and principal accuser, Klara Steinbrenner. Above all the other voices, she heard that hateful high mocking voice call out her name. Blood rose to the prisoner's face. Deeply she drew breath into her lungs, once, twice, three times, and then loosed a wail, at first high and piercing, but then wavering up and down the scale. The wail seemed to last for minutes. Through the heavy chest, the sound became transformed into something unearthly, terrifying. The four policemen hesitated, trembling, and began to loose their grasp on the chest. The crowd fell silent, straining their ears, their eyes wide. Once more the wail emanated from the chest. Now the crowd began to shout; they beat at the chest with their canes. A shower of stones battered the lid and the voices became quite menacing. By now, one end of the chest had touched the pavement. In a moment, the policemen would have fled, abandoning Katherine Kunst to a premature end, had not the provost arrived back with reinforcements and an open cart. The chest was hastily loaded, and a slow tired donkey commenced to pull its way towards the town gate.

From the low cart, Katherine was now able to make out the faces of her enemies. Everyone was there; all of her neighbors and acquaintances, and Christian too. But their terrified angry faces were scarcely recognizable. She tried to take some joy out of the effect her cry had made upon them, but instead she became increasingly uneasy. For the first time she realized the danger which threatened her. The terror which she had inspired now seized her. Who had caused that sound to issue from her throat? she wondered nervously. She felt an immense weight pressing down upon her, pushing her deep into the soft nest on which, just moments before, she had lain so comfortably. Stricken, she recognized the cold weight of Satan himself.

∴

They carried the linen chest directly into the small courtroom where all preliminary interrogations took place. Almost immediately the three examining magistrates joined the provost, who unlocked the chest and ordered the accused to stand forth. There, lying in the midst of the pillows and comforters, was the tiny shrunken body of the old lady. "Dead!" exclaimed one of the policemen. She looked quite serene there, her skin ashen, her pale hands crossed over her breast, her finery glinting in the courtroom light.

Gingerly the provost approached and bent his ear to her heart. Just then the old lady emitted a long rasping snore. In terror the provost shouted out. Before he could leap back, the awakened sleeper screamed, grabbing at his head. "The Devil, the Devil!" she shouted. Her fingernails dug into the balding skin, drawing blood. Nor did she let go until

[178]

the four policemen had seized her and pried her fingers off their superior's skull.

This outburst made everyone, including the accused, feel uneasy. The Devil, indeed, might be lurking in the very courtroom.

Now the provost began the affair by asking Katherine if she were a witch as charged. In pungent language, Katherine denied the accusation.

"Then," declared the provost, rubbing his hands together, "we shall proceed with the weeping test."

Ceremoniously, the old lady was seated upon a high stool in the middle of the courtroom while the provost stood at a lectern facing her. A great Bible was carried in by the porter, who made a show of interposing it between himself and the accused. The Bible was placed upon the lectern in front of the provost. The three black-robed magistrates approached Katherine with caution as the provost began to read.

" 'And there was a war in heaven: Michael and his angels going forth to war with the dragon; behold it was a great red dragon, having seven heads and ten horns, and upon his heads seven diadems and all the names of blasphemy. And the dragon's tail draweth the third part of the stars of heaven and did cast them to the earth.' "

Here the provost paused while the magistrates examined the eyes and cheeks of the old lady who sat very straight upon the stool like an angry young child, staring an unblinking stare of hatred at the provost.

"Dry," declared the first magistrate.

"Dry," repeated the second.

"Bone dry," snorted the third.

" 'And the dragon warred with Michael's angels. And the great dragon was cast down, the old serpent, he that is called the Devil and Satan, the deceiver of the whole world; he was cast down to the earth and his angels were cast down with him.' "

Fruitlessly the magistrates examined the old lady, looking for some sign of tearful repentance. The clear small eyes remained dry and blazing. Hurriedly the provost leafed through the Bible seeking appropriate pages. The magistrate bade the porter bring a lantern and shine it full upon the unblinking eyes of the accused, who now said: "You can plainly see that I have eternal Christ in my soul."

Crossing themselves, the magistrates backed away.

[179]

" 'He that sacrificeth unto any god,' " the voice of the provost boomed out, seeking to drown the impertinent revolt, " 'save unto the Lord only, shall be utterly destroyed. Thou shalt not suffer a sorceress to live.' Thus the Book of the Covenant has enjoined us to deal with the likes of you."

Katherine Kunst jumped down from her stool and deliberately approached the lectern. "The Book of the Covenant also says that if you afflict a widow and she cries out to God, he will hear her cry, and his wrath will kindle, and he will kill you with his sword—and all your wives will be widows and your children fatherless."

"You hear this, you hear this?" cried the provost, lifting the large book between himself and his assailant. "Katherine Kunst, your devils know me as the servant of Jesus. Don't argue against the Scriptures. Why do you remain obstinate and dry-eyed?"

"I have shed so many tears in my life that I have none left for self-serving officials. You are persecuting a God-fearing Christian because you are afraid that you too will be accused." She pointed a gnarled finger up at him.

A chill seized the provost. He began to tremble. "Take her away! Take her away! And mind you, don't let the appearance of age and weakness deceive you. Chain her fast to the cell walls. She is charged with powerful witchcraft. We want no devils freeing her in the midst of night."

∴

Katherine walked into the cell, head up, a grin screwing around her features. The two jailors greeted her warmly. After all, she and her family were now their employers, paying all expenses—food and firewood—for as long as she was imprisoned. The cell itself was small and dark, separated from the large jailor's space by a heavy iron gate. As they fastened on the ankle and wrist irons, they called her "mother." She replied: "I always said you two would end up in jail." She had known them since they were idle boys loitering around the streets of Gottwald. More than once she had boxed their ears and had chased them with a broom from her kitchen steps.

[180]

A fire blazed in the jailor's ante-room, and the table was set for a sumptuous evening repast. Quite considerately, the jailors offered her a dinner plate, which she refused. She asked them to leave her in peace.

Now Katherine's mood plunged to the depths. The cold iron on her ankles and wrists brought back that moment in the linen chest when the Devil himself had assaulted her with all of his cold metallic weight. The main trouble, she thought, was in telling the difference between the gifts of the Dark One, and the gifts of the Bright One, blessed be He. If God were all-powerful, why had he created Satan? To tempt humankind, no doubt. It was confusing enough for learned minds, let alone for the mind of an uneducated woman.

Perhaps she was a witch, as they had accused. But if she had made a pact with the Devil, she had been thoroughly cheated, that much she knew. It had been, after all, a terrible life. Her parents had boarded her out at a young age to a spinster aunt who had abused her, employing her as a servant in her midwifing and herbal trade. Her husband proved to be a sadistic thief. Her first-born child, Joachim, the only child who gave her back any tenderness, turned out to be an epileptic and a madman to boot. Joachim was probably the only human being she ever truly cared for. She could still remember holding his thrashing body during his fits, wiping the foam off his lips. It had felt like she held the very soul of the crazy world in her arms. Of her six other children, three had died in childhood, the stupid Margot had made a good marriage to her vicar, the sly and cold Heinrich had become a prosperous merchant, and Christian had achieved some notoriety as Imperial Astronomer and author of strange incomprehensible treatises on the stars. She considered her poor sick Joachim worth a good deal more than all three of her so-called respectable children. But Joachim was safely dead now.

Katherine sighed. Her life had been ruled by the Devil, who appeared to rule the rest of the world as well. She had been the victim of a bad disposition with bile, the bitter, yellow-brown and green fluid made by the liver, uppermost. That hot dry bitter disposition had led her to rail, scold, throw pots and pans and whatever other implements came to hand, attacking, always attacking. But she had never complained. Now, as she wondered if she would end in smoke and flames, her proper element—hot and dry like bile—she realized how much she loved life.

∴

Katherine Kunst remained chained to the same wall of the keep at the town gate for fourteen months, during which time an incredible amount of paperwork piled up regarding her case: a thousand pages in all, and more than half of it in the hand of her assiduous son Christian. All the papers were duly filed with the Faculty of Law at Tübingen, who deliberated for over a month on the case.

During the first two weeks of her imprisonment, her daughter Margot dutifully visited every other day, taking care to appear at odd hours when few people on the street would see her. Katherine, who understood her daughter's reluctance even better than the young woman herself, drove her away with a malicious tongue. Heinrich, Katherine's youngest, came only once, to assure himself, he declared, of her "comfort." Katherine greeted his solicitude with such laughter that he left almost immediately and never returned. Although both Margot and Heinrich had agreed to share the expenses of the jail and the defense with Christian, both became irked at the length of time the defense was taking and they ceased their aid. Life had become so pleasant for them with their mother locked up that they began to hope Katherine would go to her fate.

Only Christian remained loyal—Christian who knew that his mother had never cared for him. For a while he had thought to win her approval by his academic success, but she never forgave him for failing to win his degree in divinity. Instead he had taken a job in mathematics and astronomy and had spent his days writing treatises on the skies and producing an annual calendar of astrological forecasts. When she asked him for a personal forecast, he refused, saying that the stars determined general matters, but not particular lives or events. "That the sky does something to man is obvious enough, but what it does specifically remains hidden," he preached at her.

"And your stars have been crossed all these years, son?"

"So it would appear."

Christian was a complainer. But his injuries never interfered with his work. Once his intellect had become engaged, challenged as it had been by his mother's complicated case, Christian Kunst was indefatigable.

And Christian paid all of the bills—which mounted alarmingly. The jailors built large fires, ate enormous meals, and even hired a lady to scrub up the two rooms. Appalled, Christian demanded itemized bills. Neither jailor could write. Christian arrived at the keep armed with a measuring stick. At first the jailors thought they were in for a beating. Instead, Christian drew a meticulous plan of the jail, calculated the amount of heat needed, night and day, figured the heat yielded by one log, and demanded that the fuel consumption be rigidly limited. He himself contracted for fuel delivery. He ordered a stuffing of cracks around the barred windows and doors. He wrote out a weekly menu, for which he arranged with a local farmer, and demanded that the jailors regularly change the straw of his mother's bed. The contract which he drew up, full of figures, ran to thirty pages.

"Poor Christian," sighed the old lady, nevertheless pleased with her new straw, "you've always been bedevilled by numbers."

"Measurements, Mama, exact measurements. The noble Tycho made them possible, and your son will use them as the foundation of a system which will embrace God's entire universe."

"God the mathematics teacher, I suppose?"

"God the geometer, Mama. He who created the peaceful harmony of the skies."

"Poor boy, you are always hanging onto someone's skirts—some duke or professor, some Tycho, even the Holy Roman Emperor, who was nothing more than a degenerate madman. As for Tycho, didn't he eat himself to death?"

Christian realized that his mother understood nothing about his work and had little respect for him. Nevertheless, he continued attempting to explain to her the importance of his unending search for truth in the skies. He crouched upon a stool at the cell entrance, patiently justifying his life and his work, which had not been all that successful. First he had sought to prove that the entire universe was built upon certain perfect symmetrical solids, Pythagorean solids. Failing in this, he had proceeded to try to build the universe around the musical harmonies of the Pythagorean scale. Finally, now, while his mother was undergoing her persecution, he was writing what he considered his greatest work, an attempt to reveal the ultimate secret of the universe, employing geometry, music, astrology, astronomy, and the theory of knowledge. In this endeavor he maintained that he had found a continuous song in heavenly motions, a song perceived by the intellect, not by the ear, a song which reflected Pythagorean geometrical proportions echoing throughout the earth and the heavens.

Katherine rose up, her chains clinking. She lifted a cupped hand to her ear and tilted her head. "I'm listening, dear Christian, and I hear nothing more harmonious than the sound of a cart-wheel on paving stones." Goading him, she continued, "The provost said that you are probably a heretic."

"How would he know my beliefs?"

"He says that nowhere in the Scriptures could anyone find the nonsense you write."

"Theology has no place in science, nor does the Holy Scripture. The heavenly machine is like clockwork, governed by simple magnetic and material force."

"Then our town clock is sacred?" she asked, her eyes wide with innocence. "We should pray every time it strikes."

"So the monks believed, my dear Mama."

"And God could stop time, if he wished?"

"No. He created too perfect a machine. Just as all motions of a clock are governed by a single weight, the forces which govern the skies are in perfect numerical and geometrical proportion and proceed without end."

"Why carry on so about the skies, when down here everything has fallen to shambles?"

Christian sighed. It had been a hard, lonely decade. "At least peace reigns in the skies, Mama, and stars are not accused of witchcraft."

∴

When her son finally left her alone, Katherine was relieved. She could not stomach the idea of a divine celestial harmony revolving around somewhere up there while human lives were being destroyed daily. She was, after all, chained to a wall, guarded by two town vagrants, the object of a forty-nine point accusation, plus the charge of failure to shed tears when admonished by texts from the Holy Scripture. By now, time had disappeared for her. Every ring of the church bell sounded with an interminable echo. Ravaged by misgivings about her brutal life, she concentrated upon one object: whatever would be her final moment—the torture to come, the public burning, or triumphant vindication—she chose to show herself brave and contemptuous to her fellow townsmen. She had no tears. Indeed, all her juices had been sucked out of her by life; she was dried up, a hard old root, off which even an axe would glance harmlessly. If they did burn her, it would have to be in one of those crucibles used for refining iron.

One morning, four masked, robed figures appeared in the cell, waking Katherine. Not a word was spoken. The chains were removed. She was led through the door and down the circling stairwell. Hardly able to walk, she had to be half-carried. They continued down into a cellar and even further down into a large chamber crowded with an odd assortment of apparatus. Standing in the midst of the chamber was the provost. Next to him stood the three magistrates, and a fourth man in robes, looking more distinguished than all the others. He was the representative of the Law Faculty appointed to judge her case.

Katherine threw off the helping hands of her escort and advanced, a small figure, still wearing her fine jewelry. Her dress was clean and proper—Christian had insisted upon that.

"Do you, Katherine Kunst, admit to practising witchcraft, to having entered into a pact with the Devil? . . ." The Provost read out all the charges, one by one, glancing up each time.

Katherine stretched and yawned. The removal of the chains had exhilarated her, and, weakened though she was from her imprisonment, her mind felt clear and all of her senses tingled. She waved her hands about. She danced a little this way and that, disconcerting her escort, who, perhaps, expected her to fly up in the air and disappear.

When the provost had finished, he looked up expectantly.

"Well? What is your answer?"

"Nonsense!"

"Please reply to the charges."

"I'm not a witch and I've never had the honor of making the Devil's acquaintance."

[185]

"You realize, do you not, that if you continue in your obdurate ways we shall be constrained to torture you until you do confess?"

"Why else would you have brought me here?"

"You have one more chance."

"Get on with it."

"Executioner! Display your wares!"

One of the masked figures now threw off his cloak, took hold of Katherine's arm, and propelled her forward. In great detail he explained each of his devices: the gresillons, which crushed the tips of fingers and toes in a vice; the échelle, a rack which stretched the body violently; the tortillon, which twisted and squeezed each of the body's tender parts; the strappado, a pulley which jerked the body violently in mid-air; the Spanish boot, which squeezed the calf and broke the shin-bone in pieces; the lift, which hoisted the arms fiercely behind the back; the witch-chair, a seat of spikes heated from below, and the bed of nails, which pierced the body with heated points. As he named each, the executioner touched the affected parts of Katherine's body, describing the pain and the screams of the victim. Katherine felt like a piece of meat about to be carved by a butcher. Chills swept up her back. She swayed, feeling nauseated, and the executioner had to hold her up.

Smiling complacently at his colleagues, the provost stepped forward. Once more he shouted out the accusations and asked for her confession. "The moment you confess, Katherine Kunst, we can all leave this grisly charnel house and go to my comfortable office where I will offer you some tea, and we will witness the signing."

At the sight of the grin which spread across the official's face, strength rushed into Katherine's limbs. She tore her arm from the executioner's grasp and shouted back at the provost: "Even if you were to tear one artery after another from this poor body, I would have nothing to confess." She knelt and began to pray, "Our Father, who art in heaven . . ." The witnesses crossed themselves devoutly. The provost fell back as if he had been struck. When she had finished, she lifted her head, looking up at the damp high ceiling. "Now Lord, please make a sign if I am a witch or have ever had anything to do with witchcraft!" All the eyes in the chamber followed hers. "Make a sign, Lord!" She paused, and put her hands towards the provost. "Kill me, if you like.

Torture me. Burn me. God will reveal the truth once I am gone. He will reveal the injustice and violence that he has allowed to be done to me. God will not withdraw the comfort of the Holy Ghost and His crucified son." Her blazing eyes found the heavy-lidded, almost bored face of the representative from the Faculty of Law. He shrugged his shoulders and tapped the provost on the shoulder. The comedy was over. The accused had passed the test. She must now be released. The sentence by the faculty had been that the accused be questioned under *threat* of torture: if she persisted in her denial, she should be freed.

That evening Katherine was given over into the hands of her son Christian who took her immediately from the city of Gottwald, talking all the while about numbers, magnitudes and periodic motions by which God, the geometer, ruled the skies. Kept awake by her son's chatter, Katherine shivered in the drafty coach. Today she had triumphed by taking the name of the Lord in vain. In her heart she knew it was the Devil who ruled the world and all living creatures.

A

B

C

D

E

F

A   The provost's jail, facsimile of a wood engraving by J. Damhoudere.

B   Witches' Saḅbath, by Jacques de Cheyn II, 1565-1629, Netherlands, courtesy of The Metropolitan Museum of Art, purchase, 1962, Joseph Pulitzer bequest.

C   Limestone statue of grief, entitled "Pleurant," 15th century France, courtesy Museum of Fine Arts, Boston, Frederick Brown Fund.

D   Judges of the common tribunals, wood engraving, 16th century.

E   A German astronomer, wood engraving of the 16th century by J. Amman.

F   Question by torture, the estrapade, facsimile of a wood engraving by J. Millaeus.

G   Astronomical instrument.

G

XIII

A Green and Pleasant Land

ONE fine Sunday morning, Jack Worseley, a handsome, black-bearded cottager, his wife and six children arrived, a little late as usual, at the church of Loescroft Parish. To Jack's surprise, a crowd of his neighbors milled about outside the church door. The crowd parted to let the Worseleys through. Inside Jack could see the more prosperous members of the congregation already seated in their favored pews. The minister waited at the lectern. On the church door fluttered a neatly pinned notice. Jack was asked to read it once more, aloud, and to give his own comments upon the matters written there. Jack Worseley was considered the best-informed cottager of the parish. His neighbors took pride in his early promise as a scholar. The knowledge that his life had turned out to be one of unceasing labor with his hands, like their own, only added to their warmth for him.

The innocuous looking sheet of paper on the church door spelled out the end of a way of life which had been going on in Loescroft parish for almost a thousand years. On it, in a fine round hand, Lord Swiningdon, lord of Loescroft Manor, and others declared their intention to petition Parliament for the drainage and allotment of four thousand acres of Oatmoor Common, and the enclosure and allotment of all the surrounding common lands included by Loescroft, Harlton, Stinsley, and Fenway Parishes.

For centuries England had divided itself up into a system of commons and of common fields whereby the land—meadow, ploughland, and wasteland—and its resources were shared by its inhabitants. No one knew how this system began, or whether, in the beginning, everything had been shared equally, but over generations the shares had become unequal. The common ploughland was divided up into strips, each of which was "owned" by someone. The farmer who "owned" more strips had more rights to the common meadow and common waste, and had more power in the common council where all decisions were made: the type of crops to be planted, for example, the rotation of the fields, the date of harvest and the management of the waste. In almost every parish or group of parishes, there resided one grand man, the lord of the manor, who had somehow come into possession of the best land for his private use. In addition, the lord retained special rights over much of the common land, and could command certain services from the villagers. At Loescroft, Lord Swiningdon claimed the right of appointing a moor driver of Oatmoor Common. Once a year, the lord's driver herded the cattle browsing upon Oatmoor Common to his manor, where the lord took possession of all unidentified creatures. The lord also claimed rights of soil, including mineral rights, for what good they were—there being no discernible riches beneath that poor swamp—and the right of sport, which had yielded up many a brace of game and water fowl over the centuries.

Today, on sheets of paper tacked to church doors of all four parishes, Lord Swiningdon—and the other substantial landowners of the region —claimed another right: the right of enclosure, which, with their power in common council, they could command over their poorer neighbors.

After reading the notice aloud, Jack Worseley paused. "Enclosure," he said quietly. The crowd drew near. Inside the church, heads turned towards the door. "Do you know," his voice rose with each word, "what right our good lord is now claiming?" He threw out one arm in the direction of the village, the fields and the great marsh he loved. "The right to take that which we, our fathers, and their fathers before them have held in common, the fruits of God's rain and His sunshine, to gather it together, and portion it out so that every bit of land within our four parishes will be bound and fenced in and held in private by those who have the means to pay all the necessary expenses." He wheeled around and pointed inside the church where the prosperous farmers of the parish and their families shifted about uncomfortably on their well-worn pews. "As for the rest of us, whether or not we have rights to the common, when the bill of expenses is presented at our doors, we will be left portionless, servants and slaves to the wealthy."

The poor cottagers of Loescroft parish crowded around the orator. They waited. Unfortunately, Jack had spoken himself into a predicament. He had not prepared an adequate climax. Jack turned. He reached out, plucked the fluttering white sheet from the door, and began to tear it into strips. "Every one of these scraps, neighbors, represents a strip of our common inheritance!" he shouted, throwing the lot up into the breeze. This was greeted by a loud hurrah. Thus Jack Worseley began his short career as leader of the revolt against the enclosure of Oatmoor Commons and the common lands of the surrounding parishes.

There had always been a Worseley at Goose Cottage in Loescroft parish. Until recent times, the Worseleys had been wealthy farmers, with land throughout the commons and a powerful voice in the affairs of the parish. Village gossip had it that the family had been done in by learning—not a lot of learning, but just enough to enlist several generations in unpopular causes. One Worseley after another had ended his days in gaol under an accumulated debt of fines and lawsuits. Jack's father had sold off the last strip of Worseley land before his death, leaving nothing but Goose Cottage, a few pigs, four sheep, a cow, a horse, and a large flock of geese. Ordinarily Jack would not have inherited Goose Cottage, but both of his elder brothers, seeing what the future held for them in Loescroft parish, had disappeared. Unfortunately, along with his father's debts, Jack also inherited the family disease: he read too much.

As a younger son, Jack had been encouraged to study with the local curate and had shown such promise that there was talk about his going to London to make his way in a very different world from that of the great marsh and the low rolling hills of his home county. Instead, he found himself with an ailing mother, four younger brothers and sisters and a freely held cottage. Fortunately, the cottage title included rights to the common meadow, pasture, and waste of the parish, considerable advantages to the landless. The disappointed scholar managed to pay his father's debts and provide for his family through generous use of his common rights. The waste offered up its fern for litter and browsing, its furze and peat for fuel, acorns and mast for the swine, as well as small timber for pens and fences.

No sooner had Jack placed his younger brothers and sisters in life than he promptly married and brought six more beings into the world. He supplemented the family income by hiring himself out at harvest and planting. The women of the family took care of the rest of their needs by producing woolens piecework for local merchants. Without their common rights, however, the family could not survive. Enclosure would mean the end of Jack's independence and force him to give up Goose Cottage.

On the next Sunday, when the enclosure agent appeared to tack up the second Notice of Intention, the crowd, led by Jack, barred the way. The agent stuck his head out of the coach window, read the notice aloud and threw copies out at random before ordering the coachman to drive on. On the third Sunday, the coach was stoned and the horses stampeded before the agent even turned in at the village.

The Petition for Enclosure, however, was duly received by Parliament and referred to committee, which swiftly reported in favor of the Bill. It did no harm to the case that the senior member of the committee was brother-in-law to Lord Swiningdon, and that a series of articles began to appear in the London paper concerning the fact that the kingdom had to import millions of sterling in corn from foreign lands, while the potentially rich commons of Oatmoor district remained in waste during the summer months and under water all through the winter.

In the meantime, Jack, with the help of the aged curate who had taught him to read, formed the Committee to Save Oatmoor Commons. The Committee applied to the keeper of the record in the Augmentation Office for a report on the history of Oatmoor. After a most careful search, no citation of Oatmoor could be found in any record. In fact, it was discovered that Oatmoor had never been included within the bounds of any manor in recorded history, nor had any lords of nearby manors ever received written rights of common upon it. The custom of "usage without stint" by the inhabitants made it likely that even Lord Swiningdon's right of soil had been usurped at some recent time.

On the very day that the counter-petition drawn up by Jack's committee was submitted and summarily tabled, Lord Swiningdon's Bill of

Enclosure passed the commons. Two months later the enclosure received royal assent, and within a week, commissioners favorable to the lord and his allies descended upon Oatmoor to parcel out the land and to assess the inhabitants their share of the cost of draining and dividing up the commons. As Jack had predicted, it became obvious that the poor of the district would have to sell their rights for whatever sum their wealthier neighbors offered. They could not afford to pay the expenses of enclosure.

The disturbances could have been foretold. Straggling crowds from all four parishes marched randomly through the moor tearing down the newly erected fences. A nephew of Lord Swiningdon's appeared at one of the manor boundaries, brandishing a pistol. The cottagers disarmed him, beat him with staves and sent him scurrying back to the manor in rags. The village constables refused to take action against their neighbors, and the lord sent for the military.

Sensing a showdown, Jack Worseley organized a more ambitious protest. He organized a grand march around the entire four thousand acres of the moor in accordance with the old custom of commonage. This march would reassert the villagers' ancient rights of possession to a land which had been usurped not only by enclosure, but for hundreds of years by the assumed privilege of the lord of the manor.

Early on a Monday September morning, five hundred men, women, and children from the four parishes assembled, armed with reaping hooks, hatchets, bill hooks, and duckets. From the neighboring countryside, five hundred more sympathetic souls joined them. They set off around the seven-mile boundary of the moor, destroying every fence in their way. Worseley, playing the commanding general, admonished them to maintain perfect order and to treat everyone they encountered with polite forebearance. It was an awesome sight to see this stern troop marching with decorum through the countryside, wading through water up to their waists, cutting their way through thick brush, climbing up and down hills, and reserving their violence for the man-made fences which blocked their way. They moved in ranks with religious solemnity, marching in solidarity with their buried ancestors, asserting with their bodies their prescriptive and inalienable rights to a custom of usage without stint since before the memory of man.

It was late in the afternoon before the marchers completed their tour, returning to their place of assembly close upon the village of Loescroft. There, awaiting them, was a troop of yeomen who ringed them round. Men, women, and children, caked with mud and sweat stood listening to the Riot Act read by the captain of the guard. Not one of them moved to disperse at the captain's command.

The captain ordered one hundred of the leading men, including Jack Worseley, seized and taken to the church, where they were examined individually. Fifty, whose names had appeared on the counter-petition, were then arrested, loaded upon wagons, and sent under escort to the nearest city gaol.

It happened that one of the local fairs was in progress that day in the town. News of the arrest preceded the cavalcade of prisoners. Once in the crowded streets, the yeomen of the guard found themselves attacked by countrymen who had come to the fair. Bricks, stones and sticks were hurled from every side, accompanied by the cry, "Oatmoor forever!" The horses stampeded. The wagons overturned. Forty of the prisoners escaped.

That night, Jack Worseley stole off from Goose Cottage with his horse, his sheep, cow, a cart and his youngest son Jeremy, in search of a refuge and a more congenial place for the family to settle.

∴

Jack Worseley departed from his ancestral village full of anger and bitterness. Even if he had not been a fugitive, he would have been forced to leave in order to maintain his family and keep from having to sell his cottage, his birthright. His desertion bought his wife and children a place on the poor rolls. The pigs and geese would last them some time. Woolen piecework would keep them a good while longer; and after the swamp had been drained and the new farming begun, the older children would be able to find jobs subsidized by the poor rates. In the meantime, Jack would search for a new situation in which he could settle his family. He knew that this would not be easy. Parishes, afraid to allow potential burdens on their poor rolls, could refuse a certificate of settlement to any family, thus denying allowances for sickness and old age, and making it possible for authorities to remove the family to its original parish when work became scarce.

Two days on the road left Jack a profoundly shaken man. Never before had he been so far from home. Never had he seen so many new faces. He had expected to find a parish much like Loescroft and a village much like his own where, with his meager savings and the funds from the sale of Goose Cottage and its rights, he could purchase a somewhat poorer cottage with similar common rights. But the further he got from home, the more he realized that he and his neighbors had been living in the past. The face of the land had been altered. As far as the eye could see, hedges and fences enclosed all of nature. The large new farms, immense squares made up of former common strips, were growing crops which he had never before seen: sainfoin and lucerne for fodder; white clover and grass; and, to his amazement, great fields of root crops, turnips mainly. He understood now why the herds of sheep and cows looked so fat and glossy. These new farmers were raising livestock to sell at market as meat.

Even the roads on which Jack traveled had changed. Before, the roads had followed the sinuous courses of hills and valleys, curling around obstacles, dipping and rising, sometimes even turning into muddy waste without boundary; now the roads lanced straightway through the land on raised embankments. These roads were called turnpikes, and to go any distance on them, one had to pay fees. Rivers and streams had been connected with wonderfully constructed canals, once again following the geometer's rule. And everywhere, people and things were moving. It did not take Jack long to figure out that everyone and everything was moving either to the great cities, or away from them.

After a week of traveling, Jack began to understand that he would not easily find a refuge for himself and his family. His animals had begun to suffer from the journey. Proper pasturage, even for the night, could not be found, and his purse was beginning to empty. He could not afford the turnpike tolls. Reluctantly, he disposed of his cart, horse, sheep, and cow at a large country market. He sent his son Jeremy home with the proceeds.

As he traveled on, Jack began to suspect that he might never find another cottage with common rights attached. He missed his wife and children sorely. Finally, he decided to seek work as a laborer so that he could send for his family. Almost immediately Jack found a position. His talent with livestock was much appreciated on the new farms dedicated to raising beasts for market. But at the end of the first week, the foreman informed him that no matter how valuable he proved to be, the job would last only eleven months. The same would be true wherever he found labor. The prosperous new farmers had agreed among themselves to limit employment in this manner in order to insure that the parish poor rates would not increase. As it took a year to obtain a certificate of settlement, laborers not native to a parish could never bring their families to join them.

Jack considered it pointless to remain in a situation which would not lead to his being reunited with his family. He worked a month and then moved on. Sick with longing, he searched for a parish which would accept his family. Traveling did not agree with him, nor did his new position in life as a common laborer. Four months passed and Jack was no nearer to his goal. He took work only long enough to obtain funds to travel on in his search. Among the temporary labor on the new farms almost all the talk was of relatives who had gone north for jobs in the mines or in the great cities which were growing up there. Jack drifted north. Over every hill he saw fences and hedges. He came to mining villages, but he did not bother to inquire for work. He had read in the journals about conditions in the mines, and he had no desire to see his family thus degraded.

Finally he came to his first city. In the distance he saw the chimney stacks, great billowing creatures which rose up, dwarfing even the church steeples. As he trudged down the road, he made out the mills—buildings larger than any he had ever seen. At last he entered the dense crowded streets of the city itself. Barely able to breathe, assaulted on every side by creatures who seemed intent upon tearing the clothes from his back, he felt as if he had slipped into the muck of the swamp —except that everyone in this great mass of humanity looked, to his country eye, gorgeously dressed. And they all spoke with a swiftness and elegance which shamed his country speech. Jack Worseley, the grand orator of the Lion and the Lamb, spoke not a single word in the city.

At the same time, great excitement welled up within this proud cottager. Never before had there been so much to read: billboards, signs, advertisements, notices, handbills and three different journals, one of them all the way from London. For two days he marched back and forth through the filthy, littered streets, gazing and gawking, listening and trying to understand what this new world might offer him. Instinctively, he knew that if he had arrived here thirty years earlier he would have found his way. He even felt that, with the help of his beloved wife and children and just a little money, he might make a place for himself here. But the shock of his departure from Loescroft and the demeaning voyage seemed to have broken Jack's spirit. After two days, he fled north, still hoping to find a hidden parish which had not been swallowed by enclosure.

During three weeks of weary hiking, from every hilltop Jack saw only more hedges and more fences. He became obsessed with his search, obsessed with walking. He ate very little. His beard and his hair grew unkempt; his clothes, with which he had always taken great pains, now grew filthy. He mumbled to himself in his extreme loneliness. It was in such a state that Jack Worseley came upon a great expanse of unfenced, yet well tended land.

∴

The high road upon which Jack walked wound through gentle rolling hillsides. The absence of fences struck Jack's eye first, and the quality of the soil. His heart leaped; perhaps he had found a new home for his family. His attention became rivetted upon a strange structure in a deep wide valley. It was a very large bridge in a peculiar style which seemed faintly familiar to him. First there was the bridge proper, with five arches, four small and one large; then there was an elaborate balustrade; and finally, rising high above the bridge was a strange roof held up by columned arches. For a long time Jack stood, gazing down at the odd structure. It appeared to span perfectly dry land. Below it, he saw gangs of men at work around a series of small ponds. Other men appeared to be doing something on distant hillsides.

Drawn to the vision of unfenced land and the curious bridge, Jack Worseley set off down the hillside to find out what place he had come to.

As he walked, he remembered where he had seen similar constructions: in very old books in the curate's library, books written in Latin. He wondered that there were no fences to keep in the herds of cows which browsed peacefully on the meadowland surrounding the ponds. As he arrived at the valley bottom, he came to a man-made ditch combined with an embankment, an arrangement which made a very effective fence to the grounds, preventing cattle from straying. The curate had mentioned such hidden barriers in describing certain great European battles of the past. Jack could never have imagined the ditch-embankments put to use so cleverly.

Jack pulled himself up the embankment and stepped into a meadowland which had been planted, here and there, with saplings. He wondered why anyone would plant trees in the midst of a meadow, or build an elaborate ancient bridge over dry land. He came to a place from which he could see the sweep of hills surrounding the valley. Jack had seen many a similar hill in his home county: bare, eroded hills, having been logged out many years before to provide timber for England's great fleets. Just as in the meadow, whole gangs of workers busied themselves up on the hillsides, planting saplings and seedlings among the few remaining trees. As Jack rounded a small copse, a rising expanse capped with a magnificent castle met his eye. Another gang of men appeared occupied with destroying a large formal garden which surrounded the castle. They tore down geometrical hedges, cut down alleys of pine, dug out flower beds and knocked down balustrades and steps.

Jack could now see that the workmen in the meadow were engaged in damming up the ponds. By now the foreman of that group noticed the intruder and approached, demanding to know what he was doing on private grounds.

"I don't know," replied Jack, who then stepped around the foreman, making his way towards the dam.

"Here now," exclaimed the foreman, "where do you think you're going?" He signalled to two of the workers to take Jack prisoner.

"A lake!" Jack exclaimed, as his arms were seized. "Why are you making a lake here?"

So amazed was he by the idea that anyone should want to create a lake in the middle of a meadow, that he hardly noticed he was being hurried up the valley towards the great house. The bridge would span the lake then, he decided, but why the bridge should have been so elaborately constructed remained a mystery.

Soon Jack found himself standing in front of the stables, from which there issued a harried elderly man in neat working clothes, a sheaf of papers under his arm. As the official questioned him, Jack realized how he must look: an emaciated figure, with torn clothing, unkempt beard and hair wildly shooting off his head in every direction. He could be arrested and thrown into jail for trespassing and vagrancy. He stood up straight, took off his cap and attempted to explain. He was a poor cottager, he said, who had been dispossessed. Seeking work, he had lost his way and wandered for several days until he had come upon this place.

At that moment, a party of gorgeously attired gentlemen and one lady galloped up. No sooner had the lords and the lady dismounted than one of the gentlemen ran over to see to the unloading of a pack horse which had accompanied the party. The luggage consisted of a number of canvases and easels. The gentleman wore a curious costume which resembled an ordinary gardener's clothes, but was made up in finer cloth, corduroy and velvet, and fitted exquisitely. He looked to Jack like a painting master come to give instruction to the owners of this grand manor.

The party began to walk towards the castle when the "artist" gentleman stopped in front of Jack. "What have we here?"

"Just a vagrant soul," murmured the estate official.

"But he's the perfect image we need. I couldn't have created anything better. Does he want employment?"

"Employment?" With wondering eyes, everyone gazed at poor Jack Worseley, and then back at the "artist" gentleman.

"Have you taken leave of your senses, man?" asked the principal lord in a rough voice.

The lady, however, laid a finger upon his forearm. "Obviously, my dear, he's wanted for the cave."

"Perfectly correct, Milady," said the "artist" gentleman. "This interesting derelict shall be our hermit. "

At the furthest reaches of his fancy, Jack could never have imagined that one day he would become a hermit—that he would sit cross-legged at the entrance of a cave, a cunningly comfortable little cottage set into the side of a hill, gazing upon the heavens and the stately grounds of a castle from which issued a brave company of lords and ladies, out for a picnic on the western heights.

"What is that?"

"Rather who?"

"Oh that is our hermit," Milady would answer casually. "He's been there forever."

In reality, Jack did not have to remain in the cave except when important visitors came to Stouringham Castle. The rest of the time, he functioned as all-around handyman for Master Capacious Kent, the gentleman who had discovered him. Master Kent served as landscape architect in charge of the renovation of the grounds of Stouringham Castle. From the first day of his employment as hermit, Jack had done his utmost to curry the favor of Master Kent, for in this amiable gentleman Jack saw the means to salvage his life as well as the Worseley name. When Master Kent left Stouringham for London, where his principal offices were located, Jack planned to be in his train.

The men became friends from the day that Master Kent discovered Jack's histrionic abilities and his penchant for reading. Jack suggested that he be allowed to speak to the guests in an oracular tone about Master Kent's theories. After all, Jack observed shrewdly, the noble visitors to Stouringham Castle could very easily become Master Kent's next clients. Delighted at Jack's canniness, Master Kent began a general course of instruction by which he imparted to his hermit both the fundamental theological basis of his art and certain practical matters in the promotion of his business enterprise. Jack poured over the pamphlets and tracts provided liberally by his teacher and soon ventured to pronounce a few pregnant sentences to the curious guests of the castle.

"What do you do all day, Hermit?" they would ask.

"I contemplate God's greatest book: Nature."

"And what do you see?"

"Grass, trees, and water; for in them, with my natural faculties, I can read God's revelation. Everything artificial has been erased from my mind by my strict regime and solitary life, just as everything artificial has been removed from this glorious landscape we see spread out before us. This land has been restored to its original purity, and from it, the impressions flow to my mind in direct communication with God. Down in the meadow, the grass grows freely, the clumps of trees spring up just as their seeds might have fallen at creation; up along the heights, great forests rise as they did before God made man; while down the undulating slopes flow pure streams in their original sinuous attempt to reach the lake below. Everything here at Stouringham is in balance as God created it in the beginning. Heavenly equilibrium has been restored and the savage soul is calmed."

In every speech Jack delivered, God, reason, nature, grass, trees, and water were joined in a satisfying whole. The hermit conducted the visitors on short hikes, to show them favorable perspectives of the countryside which had been painstakingly created by Master Capacious Kent. Jack took care to point out the progress of Master Kent's ambitious plans. Down below, the workers had finally completed the dam and closed the sluice gate. The flooding took almost a week to complete, and then willows, alders and osiers were planted around the margin. Up towards the castle, the formal gardens had given way to a charming confusion of meandering walks. Overgrown cul-de-sacs were cultivated for secluded tête-à-têtes, and rose arbors conducted happy visitors to a hidden bank over a rock-strewn stream which had been carefully sculpted by Master Kent's laborers.

The landscape architect was so pleased with Jack that not long after his arrival he entrusted him with a more ambitious project: the collection of masonry, stones and timber from the various ruins which lay in the neighborhood. When Jack inquired the purpose of this odd task, Master Kent smiled mysteriously, but only pointed out the exact location next to the main entrance drive where Jack was to pile the rubble.

After several weeks, the heap of moss-covered stones and rotted beams had grown to considerable proportions. One day Master Kent appeared as Jack unloaded his cart. The landscape architect set up his easel some yards below, and placed upon it a finished canvas. He beckoned to Jack. "Here, Hermit Worseley, you will see the purpose of your labors."

On the canvas Jack saw a finely wrought landscape with Stouringham Castle in the distance, just as it actually stood from their vantage point.

But in the foreground of the painting, next to where Jack's rubble lay, there stood the mouldering ruins of an ancient fortification.

"This is what I wish you to build for me, sage of Goose Cottage. When it is completed, the renovation of Stouringham Castle will be done and I shall take my leave."

Jack had seen many strange things since his arrival, but none so startling as a deliberately built ruin. "What's the point?" he questioned. "What good will it do anyone? At least the great lake in the lower meadows has improved the pasturage ten-fold. The clumps of trees clustered here and there through the cleared land will provide shade for the grazing livestock. The oak and beech stands on the heights will one day provide valuable timber for ships and houses." Jack could even see the point of destroying the elegant geometrical gardens surrounding the house. They had required an immense staff of gardeners. The carefully wrought disarray which had supplanted the old gardens needed very little upkeep, and still remained pleasing to the eye and comfortable for retreat and isolation. But to deliberately construct a ruined fortification, here on the main formal approach to the castle, appeared perverse to the cottager.

"My dear colleague," said the painterly architect. "Nature is but a canvas upon which a landscape must be designed. As in painting, so styles in Nature change, and we must change with the times. In my youth, because I attacked the formal geometric views of the last century, I was considered a radical. I tore down venerable lanes of trees which I considered too straight. I ripped out hedgerows which imposed too rigid an order upon the generous profusion of our common Mother. I carved sinuous banks for my ponds and lakes, and made sure that every stream moved like a snake down the hillsides. I was quite the rage, and still am in fashion, but recently I have been attacked by the up-and-coming youngsters. They think my work too gentle, innocuous, lacking in deep feeling and in profundity. If we are to continue to be successful, we must change with the times—but not too much. The great estate owners will want a caress of the New, but not the clutch of Revolution."

And so, with the help of whatever farmhands were free from day to day, Jack Worseley set about constructing a ruined fortification. Knowing that this would be his last opportunity to impress Master Kent, Jack took great pains with his task. Here and there, on his own initiative, he made additions—a blasted arch, a cross tilting wildly, a cannon barely visible in the high grass. The completed ruins turned out to be a perfect evocative success. When Master Capacious Kent left Stouringham, Jack Worseley, with beard and hair trimmed and a new tailored wardrobe, accompanied him.

∴

It took more than a year before Jack Worseley had saved up enough money to hire a lawyer to clear up the charges against him at Loescroft parish. When that was done, he removed his family from Goose Cottage to London, where he continued to work for Master Capacious Kent. Jack was careful, however, not to let go of the ancient seat of his family. He leased it to a local farmer at a good rate and admonished his children to hold onto that small piece of land. "For," as he often said, "land is the only possession which will never lose its value." He still believed that ownership of Goose Cottage preserved his right to the Oatmoor Common. He had faith that one day the great theft of enclosure would be reversed, and that the land of England would be returned to all the people.

In the meantime, he thrived in the employ of Master Kent, who found in Jack the quality of a true, loyal and independent countryman. Jack never counted the hours of his work, nor did he question wages. What he did, he did painstakingly, like a true craftsman. At his employer's bidding, he familiarized himself with all of the work and theories of the revolutionary youngsters in the field of landscape architecture. He studied the fashionable romantic Italian and French paintings which had provided the stimulus for the new school of feeling and romance. Master Kent even sent him on a trip to Italy to look at paintings and to experience the dizzying effect of the Alps at first hand.

Capacious Kent watched the progress of his protege with particular pleasure. He understood only too well the suffering of the poor yeomanry of England upon which his own art prospered. "Someone," he told Jack, "usually the poor, has to pay for progress." It was little enough, he realized, but in Jack he felt that he was helping to right the wrong a bit. He was particularly happy, one day, to put into Jack's hands the opportunity to redress his grievances in an even more substantial way. Master Kent had received a commission from the new Lord Swiningdon of Loescroft Manor. The old lord had died, and the title had gone to a distant nephew. With great good humor, Master Kent urged Jack to take on the full responsibility for the task, loaning him his fine carriage and several servants for an unlimited amount of time.

Jack set off in grand style with his son Jeremy, who had grown to be a handsome, accomplished young gentleman. At Loescroft Manor Jack was appalled at what he found. Once enclosure had been achieved, the old Lord Swiningdon had been too ill to oversee his lands. A series of incompetent managers had left the estate in sorry condition. The first attempt to drain the great swamp had ended disastrously, with the flooding of many acres of valuable farmland. Four-fold field rotation had been instituted half-heartedly and then abandoned because of the resistance of the laborers to change. To make up for the dwindling income of the estate, the managers had sold off tracts of forest to lumber merchants. The bare hills had begun to erode badly.

Jack could see that he had his work cut out for him. The young lord wanted to be intimately involved in the renovation of his newly acquired estate. Arrogant by nature and education, he wished to be the genius who recreated the family fortune and style. He let Jack know that he was mightily disappointed that the famous Master Kent had not come himself.

"Ahhh," said Jack slowly. "Master Kent is getting on in years. He reserves his energies for certain more settled projects: the ancient lands which must be preserved. You said in your letter that you required the most modern and up-to-date plan, did you not?"

"Precisely."

"And besides, Lord Swiningdon," Jack nodded gravely, "if I may be frank?"

"Certainly."

"We must be honest in our profession. There are other less-established firms who seek to gull their customers into vast expenditures by flattering their pretensions. I could empty your pockets swiftly if you want to play charades. While Loescroft Manor is a pretty little estate, it is no Stouringham Castle, nor would you be well served if I pretended so."

Such honest conversation was not easy for the young lord to bear. Reluctantly he agreed to employ Jack at least in the production of an initial report and prospectus.

"Let us first take a turn around your land," suggested Jack, "to get an impression of its peculiar character. Some land is grand, other land savage; then there is the sprightly landscape, the melancholy, the horrid, or the beautiful. Wherever one of these characters prevail, our job will be to strengthen its effect."

And so Jack took the young master for an exhausting ride. They started and stopped, mounted and dismounted and contemplated. Jack directed his son to make countless sketches. The nervous young lord snapped at his men, ordering them about, but took great pains to be polite to Jack and Jeremy, who seemed to hold his entire future in their hands.

As the day proceeded, Jack became increasingly reflective and removed. At last he had returned to Oatmoor Common, the great marsh and rolling hills of the land he loved, but he heard no trumpets, he saw no bolts of a just God's lightning which would overturn the usurpation of common rights. On this ride he allowed himself to admit that nothing he or his son could do would turn back the events of hundreds of years which had led to the end of their fellowship with this particular piece of land. They might own Goose Cottage, and a few feet around it, but nothing more. The living Worseley roots which had drawn sustenance from Oatmoor's soggy earth for generations were severed.

At the end of the day, still on their horses, the three men looked over the expanse of Loescroft Manor.

"Lord Swiningdon," Jack spoke in a weary voice, "the overwhelming impression which your estate conveys is one of melancholy."

"Melancholy?" repeated the lord, startled.

"A deep, let me say, profound melancholy. Your hills are not high enough, nor sculpted in such a way that they could convey grandeur."

Taken aback, the lord protested that he thought his hills savage and beautiful.

"No, these hills are sad, sad hills. For you I shall devise gloomy settings in which your friends can brood with great satisfaction. Little

[209]

corners with views of ruined cottages—not abbeys, not fortifications—but cottages. Here at Oatmoor, the feeling is one of the fate of common men—all men."

"Melancholy?" The young lord inquired again, a trifle cast down.

"It's all the rage on the continent, and London is just beginning to catch wind of it. You and Loescroft shall be in the forefront."

"Profound melancholy," murmured the lord, sighing a bit. "I like the sound of it. Life is certainly no trivial thing like it was in the early days of this century when people thought they had solved the riddle of the universe."

"You are very quick to understand. To begin with, the pretty little garden which surrounds the manor house must go. The cornerstone of the new garden shall be a tomb."

"A tomb? Whose tomb?"

"Surely there's someone dead in your family? Your uncle is, I know."

"I wouldn't want his tomb in my garden, I can tell you."

"An ancestor then?"

"They were a pretty undistinguished lot."

"Your parents?"

"They didn't even have a title," said the lord, and then caught himself up short. "I mean, they preferred their own churchyard—pious folk, both."

Jack lapsed into his saddle, brooding.

"What about a child?" said Jeremy, who had hardly spoken all day.

"Ah ha!" exclaimed Jack. "Nothing is more melancholy than the tomb of a beloved child."

"But I've only just married," protested Lord Swiningdon.

"Perhaps," suggested Jack, "it would be appropriate to provide eternal shelter for one of the poor child souls of one of the humble farmers or gardeners of the village?"

Lord Swiningdon's eyes narrowed. He looked appraisingly at Jack's wide-eyed and innocent face. "A monument to those who labor faithfully." The lord smiled, nodding his head with satisfaction.

Jack sighed. Often he found his new profession trivial—downright silly: all this business about melancholy and terror and grandeur. But Master Kent and all of his kind, and Jack too, in his small way, were involved in something of a miracle. This tired England which had been proceeding to a dismal ruin, trees cut down, hills eroded and soil depleted, was now being revived. The absurd ruins and quaint little cottages they fabricated would disappear; the terrifying gorges which they had created would mellow. The wrongs of the poor villager, the poor small farmer would not be righted in any future he could foresee. But in several generations, the trees which they planted, the meadows which they revived and the fields, would bloom. England would become a green and pleasant land once more.

A

B

C

D

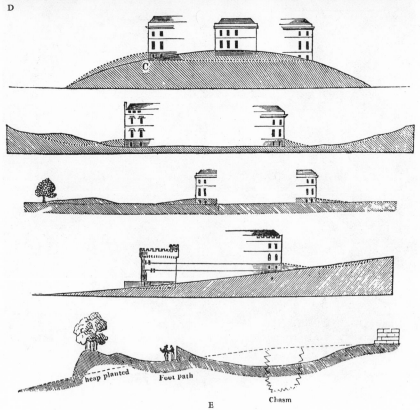

C

heap planted   *Foot Path*   *Chasm*

E

F

XIV

We Have Got
Done Praying!

To find the bones of his father in the land of the Golden Mountain, Hung Jin left the Middle Kingdom, the land of China, and voyaged across the sea. As his ship came in sight of land—a series of rounded hills falling to the water amidst jagged rocks—the young man pondered the substantiality of the Golden Mountain where he was to work for two years in payment for this journey. In his country, the center of the earth and only residence of human beings, the land ahead—rocks, sand and earth—was looked upon as a shadowy realm to be avoided at all costs. Imperial law still decreed death as the punishment for this voyage.

If all being resided in the Middle Kingdom, wondered Hung Jin as his ship came to anchor, does one carry that being with him out into this wilderness of non-being? Back in Hong Kong harbor, the few travelers who had been to the Golden Mountain seemed tainted by their experience. Their tales of rivers and forests, snow-capped mountains, steam monsters rolling upon iron rails, and painted savage Indians had sounded like the figments of childish imagination. But as the voyage proceeded, these men and their stories had taken on substance, as had the boards of the ship and the flesh of the foreign sailors. Standing on deck after two months in the hold, dizzy from the fresh air and blinded by the light, Hung Jin felt himself lose substance.

Three days later, Hung Jin departed on a ferryboat up the bay towards the mountains where he was destined to work for the railroads. He had chosen this labor deliberately because it was located near the scene of his father's death. As the boat wound its way through the meanders of the delta above the bay, the young man marveled at the balance of his great adventure. He had come from a village high in the hills near the mountains and had embarked from a thriving city on the delta of great rivers; he had boarded his ship from a port in the midst of a grand bay, had sailed across the ocean and touched land in another bay; now he was proceeding up a delta towards the hills and mountains of this new land. It was almost as if he had passed into a mirror of his previous existence. And yet everything had been strangely transformed. The delta of his homeland teemed with craft of every size and shape; its shores were cut by countless canals and creeks, on the banks of which rose settlements, villages, orchards, graveyards, shrines and pagodas, plantations of sugar cane, rice and bamboo. Today, Hung Jin saw only a flat, misty emptiness on either side of the boat. Meanders and swamps stretched for miles with nothing but occasional flocks of birds, a small hut now and then, and sometimes a single human figure. Hung Jin was happy to discover that the world of the Golden Mountain was an empty world, half-finished. He would be able to search for his father, unhampered by so many bodies and souls, so many ages of restless presences that filled the Middle Kingdom and had weighed down upon his youth.

At the Sacramento landing, a representative of the Yan Wo Company met him and directed him to the railroad station. A train waited to carry him and a troop of other newcomers from the Middle Kingdom into the mountains where they would work. At the station, none of them were prepared for the sight of the locomotive gleaming at the head of the train, smoke trailing up into the air from its great round stack. Never before had they seen such an object.

"A monster!" exclaimed one of his companions.

"A steam monster," sighed another in admiration.

"A steam God," said a third, and they all clustered about the engine, curiously examining the wheels and rods.

High above, the engineer looked out at them. With a grin he pulled a lever by his side. A great blast sounded out, frightening the laborers away from the machine. Even in his fear, Hung Jin laughed at the wonderful noise.

[218]

A few minutes later they climbed onto open flatcars and the journey began. The steam whistle blasted again and the sound penetrated Hung Jin's soul, releasing within him a joyful surge. The power of the engine traveled down through the cars, filling his body with a sense of its own strength. Neither he nor his companions could keep from smiling as they began to move through the countryside at a greater speed than any of them had ever traveled. It felt as if the world which moved so quickly was theirs to hold by virtue of this magnificent human invention. Every now and then the engineer pulled his lever, sending forth the grand noise of his whistle.

They crossed over a wide river, swollen by the autumn rains. A crude sign declared the name of the water: The American River. Hung Jin shivered. His father had helped to build the strong bridge which bore them up. The youth reproached himself for having forgotten his mission, even for a few minutes. He rubbed his palm remembering the calloused hand of his father, clasping his own hand when his father had set off to recoup the fortune of the clan. His father had been a proud man who seldom displayed his emotion, but at that parting, the older man had suddenly put out both arms and embraced him. Arcade Creek, a large sign proclaimed, designating a few raw buildings: Hung Jin was traveling to meet his father on the very tracks which his father had laid. Soon they passed Junction and began to climb. As they did, the land rose and fell away in powerful long swells. Here and there ancient weathered rocks surfaced through the yellow brown grass.

The chill of the coming winter swept over the travelers suddenly as they rose into the Sierra foothills. Hung Jin put on a jacket which the Company had provided—adding to his debt. He had been warned that he would be soon working in snow. Lucki'y, he was accustomed to the cold winds of his plateau village. But the lowlanders who accompanied him crowded together in misery, pounding one another to keep warm.

Now the forests began, filling the canyons on either side of the tracks. Below, the river rushed through narrow rock-strewn gorges. Pockets of snow lay in shady depressions all along the hillsides. The clarity of the air seemed to magnify distant objects. A sigh went up as the passengers caught their first sight of the snowy mountain peaks. Once again Hung Jihs' heart grew large with his freedom. Ahead lay a whole land of mountains, a universe of peaks which would be his home. The sky, washed and pale all day, now darkened to an intense blue. Higher and higher they climbed above the river. Great granite slabs littered the hillside. Soon they were riding along an immense cliff which towered above them and fell away steeply just beyond their tracks. The laboring engine stopped. The passengers were given permission to get down. Ahead, near the engine, a large sign faced the tracks. Hung Jin walked forward to read the words: Cape Horn. He bowed his head. This cliff was his destination. His father had died here.

A group of well-dressed passengers gathered around the engineer, who explained how the ledge had been blasted by crews lowered from the precipices above. More than a thousand feet below, glints of sun reflected off the river snaking through the granite canyon. Snow littered the hillside, and its white was repeated in the white water which fell through the rocks. Sensing his father nearby, Hung Jin walked down the tracks behind the train. He knelt, taking a handful of crushed ballast in his hands and letting it trickle to the earth. He passed his hand over the ties, the cold metal of the rail, thinking that he could feel his father's touch on these objects. He longed to call out his father's name.

Hung Jin, his sisters, brothers, and mother had been able to discover little about his father's death. They knew only that an accidental explosion had occurred and the body had been lost down the mountainside. No one had found the remains to give them proper burial. Hung Jin's contract stated that he had to work nine months before he could spend a week devoted to his search. The whistle sounded and Hung Jin was obliged to mount the flatcar again. Hung Jin sent a prayer up to T'ien, Heaven, the Law of Life and Righteousness, to guard his father's spirit and to care for him so that he might return.

As the train rolled forward in a series of heavy jolts, Hung Jin repeated the name, Cape Horn, over and over to himself. It intrigued him that someone had thought to name a mountain of granite, Cape Horn. Before his father's death, while he studied for the civil service examinations, he had worked in the foreign compound where he had learned a fair amount of English. When he had begun to understand the language, it amazed him that the devils would seek to name the world just as his own people had, and that the foreigners had succeeded, using only a very few small letters, ingeniously arranged and rearranged to form all the meanings that his own language pictured so elaborately. He thought the English letters rather ugly signs, but effective, like a small well-trained army capable of subduing the world. Cape Horn, he repeated, a cape of granite jutting out into the sky over which human beings had managed to blast a passage.

They passed Gold Run, a place his father had never reached, and Emigrant Gap. At Cisco the rails ended in a vast yard of tracks, warehouses, barracks, and shops. The town itself was a logging and lumbering center, the products of which were now almost exclusively used by the railroad. The Yan Wo Company representative who met Hung Jin assigned him to a work crew on the Summit Tunnel and directed him to follow a pack train on its way there. In the clearings, the bright afternoon sun melted the snow, thickening the track into a muddy mire; in the shade of the forests, the snow froze to a slippery crust. Overhead, white fleecy clouds rose into gigantic shapes and blue-black thunderheads gathered, giving promise to a new snowfall.

The entire mountainside was alive with work crews, thousands of men, as far as Hung Jin could see, almost to the summit. To his surprise, most of them were men from the Middle Kingdom. They were clearing a two-hundred-foot right-of-way to the entrance of the summit tunnel, cutting down great trees, grubbing out stumps with picks and shovels and even teams of oxen. Now and then a cry of warning echoed out over the mountainside, followed by a great blast. The explosions so frightened Hung Jin that he found himself walking very close to the last mule in line, rubbing up against its side. To the right, to the left, ahead and behind, the young man heard the language of his own people mingled with the sounds of chopping, sawing, and blasting. It was as if, miraculously, after his arduous voyage, he had been returned to some northern province of his own land.

The steam whistle at the summit came from a small locomotive called the Black Goose which had been shorn of its wheels and fittings, bolted onto a platform, and hooked to a hoist. The engine raised and lowered men and materials into a ninety-foot-deep shaft at the center of the summit so that the bore could be worked at from the middle as well as from both ends. All through the blizzards of that winter, Hung Jin worked down in one of the central shafts, a pure granite cavern which grew slowly east and west each week. At first he hauled debris to the hoist. Later he learned to drill the tough granite with a cast-iron drill, insert a charge, stop the hole, cut and set the fuses. He worked with wax stopping up his ears. The deadened sounds heightened the sense that he had been interred, that he had entered the heart of earth in search of his father's ghost. At the beginning he had been afraid when he descended into the center of the mountain, expecting the spirits to destroy him and the others for trespassing on their domain. But as he learned to use explosives, he felt the balance of power shift to him. If a spirit threatened, he would blast it to pieces, just as he blasted granite.

And then one day he heard of a master mason at the eastern heading who had worked the entire Cape Horn job. This man was reportedly from a village close to his. Hung Jin was sure that this mason would have information about his father. Still, the young man made no attempt to contact him. He was afraid to find out the details of the events. He felt almost as if his ignorance might keep his father alive. Since his arrival in this strange land, he had never once mentioned his father's name aloud, and as the days went on he began to suspect that his father's spirit would revenge itself upon him for his cowardice and neglect. Whatever the terms of his contract, he should have buried his father when he first arrived. Every day his fear grew. As he set his charges, he trembled. Only when he resolved to ask for a transfer to the east heading and to seek out the master mason did his fear subside.

At the east heading, great snow drifts had piled up, forming a huge snow dome, lit by lanterns and tallow dips. The laborers reached their work through long snow tunnels. All grading work had long ago ceased, but the masons continued to dig their way down to the retaining walls which were being built to shore up the canyon entrances to the tunnels. The masons spent their days cutting and fitting the intricate jigsaw pieces of granite into a durable support for the track. By chance Hung Jin was put to work with the very mason who had worked at Cape Horn. But the young man did not identify himself.

In the snow tunnels, Hung Jin learned his new trade. His hands worked swiftly and well. He began to dream of the moment when the two center headings would meet the bores from either end and Number 6 would be a single tunnel through which the train would run, pulled by the magnificent steam god. As the winter passed, he learned more about why the railroad was being built. For him, the essential goal was to join together two great oceans so that men would be able to travel by train from one shore to the other. This idea caught his fancy. At home he had often wondered where he would end up if he kept walking westward. No one in his village knew anything about the lands which lay beyond the boundaries of the Middle Kingdom. His tutors in Canton had understood only a little more, and were afraid to discuss the subject. Here, in this new and empty continent, men were afraid of nothing. For Hung Jin, the railroad began to represent his own freedom, and he worked with great enthusiasm. Every now and then the earth shook mildly with the dim detonations from within the mountain as men forced their way through the solid granite. Otherwise there was only the sound of dripping water, the sound of metal upon granite, chipping, cracking, tamping. At different times of the day the snow cavern in which he worked had a blue cast, at others a yellow-white. On warm days between blizzards, a hazy light sometimes filtered down from the surface where the snow roof thinned. Soon it would be time for Hung Jin to travel back to Cape Horn.

The spring thaws began. All night Hung Jin could hear water melting and rushing down the mountainside. Now and then in the distance would come the thunderous sound of a snow avalanche. One morning, on the way through the snow trenches to work, Hung Jin heard a great whoosh just behind him and then a tremendous shudder. He turned to see the entire snow tunnel slipping downhill. He had time to reach out and grab only the coat of the master mason, pulling him free from the slide. Twelve others behind him disappeared. Weeks later, they found the bodies below, still frozen, still holding to their picks and shovels. The master mason expressed his gratitude with one embarrassed bow, but when the appointed week arrived during which Hung Jin would return to Cape Horn, the older man expressed his regrets at Hung Jin's sorrow. He had recognized Hung Jin's resemblance to his father on the first day the young man reported to work. And then, almost as if it were an afterthought, he cautioned Hung Jin that he should not expect to find much among the rocks below the granite cliff.

The next morning Hung Jin hiked down to Cisco and journeyed back along the track on an empty supply train. Some miles below Cape Horn, he left the train and made his way back along the course of the river to the base of the cliff. It was a bright sunny day. He could hear the snow melting, running downhill in pouring rivulets, swelling the river. Patches of black earth and bright green grass appeared from moment to moment. The hike over the soggy earth was not an easy one. Often he plunged to his hips in soft snow. Where the river overflowed its banks, he had to wade through icy water. It was late afternoon before he came in sight of the great granite wall of Cape Horn. High above, he could make out the cut for the rails. He made camp at the bend of the river and ate a meager meal.

That night Hung Jin prowled along the river, taking sights into the sky, trying to find a spot sheltered from the influences of evil stars. Early the next morning, he was up before dawn, and by midmorning he had located a small rise perfectly situated for the repose of his father's remains. He rejoiced that he had been fortunate in his misfortune. This place of uninhabited hills, with a snaking watercourse, provided perfect male and female shapes of ground and many lucky ravines, so that the currents of earth's power would pass on the correct sides of the tomb. After carefully diagramming the outlines of the proposed tomb, Hung Jin moved along the base of the cliff, trying to locate the approximate spot where the master mason had witnessed the accident. The young man did not believe he would find the body of his father, but he felt it necessary to make the attempt. He climbed as high as he could up the granite slabs. Slipping on the moss and fungus, he searched the crevices for bones, stuffing whatever he found into a sack he carried at his belt. For two days he crisscrossed his way along the foot of the granite cliff, covering the ground all the way to the river in case an animal had dragged the remains for some distance. Knowing nothing about bones, he made no attempt to sort through his discoveries. He did not find a complete skeleton of any creature.

On the third day, Hung Jin took his tools to the rise where the tomb was to be built. Now he put his new knowledge of masonry to use, chipping and splitting, tamping and planing until he had assembled a great armchair of granite, with a beautiful rock, streaked with green, as the back. The opening at the low end of the tomb pointed over the sweeping curve of the river where the water bubbled over a shelf of stones and boulders. As Hung Jin worked, he heard a melodic song. Turning, he saw a bird dancing about the boulders in the middle of the icy stream. It shook itself, sang, wobbled about, and strode full into the water until it submerged, only to reappear some paces further on, wobbling and singing. Charmed, Hung Jin thanked the creature and asked it to return often to amuse the spirit of his father and to keep it at peace.

When the tomb was ready and its floor had been dug out, Hung Jin returned to his campsite. Down through the boulders he climbed to a still backwater where he washed himself thoroughly. When he was clean, he donned a white suit which he had kept at the bottom of his basket since the day of his departure from home. Fastening a white cloth around his head, he began to cry out a sorrowful song. From his basket he now took a great colorful banner and fastened it to a sapling which he had cut. He hoisted his basket to his shoulder, and holding the banner aloft he began to march, as if he were in a procession, towards the tomb of his father. Three times he proceeded around the hillock on which the tomb was situated. Then he mounted it, setting the sapling into the earth. The banner fluttered in the breeze. Now he emptied the bag of bones he had gathered into the grave. There were bones of every size and shape, the bones of animals and perhaps of men. Hung Jin stood above the open grave, begging his father to forgive him this indignity. All creatures had been made by T'ien, he explained; and all deserved Heaven's blessing. For some time he stood above the open grave, chanting. When he had finished his prayers, he knelt and tore up three tufts of new grass which he threw down upon the bones. He filled the grave and completed the burial by covering the entire inside of the tomb with carefully fitted pieces of granite.

For the rest of the day, Hung Jin made model houses, horses, oxen, a crude locomotive, and money out of paper. These he reverently placed in a ring near the tomb. As darkness fell, he stood, opened a wine jug, and poured a few drops over the tomb. After taking a long swallow, he lit the paper figures and watched them burn, sending their essences to keep company with the soul of his father and the other creatures which the tomb embraced. Before leaving, Hung Jin placed several tins of food, a full bottle of wine, sprigs of incense, and three strips of red and white paper, held down by stones, within the arms of the tomb, to show that this grave was cared for tenderly by the family of the deceased. Hung Jin bade his father and his father's companions farewell, and made his way back to the rails.

∵

Truckee, Reno, Wadsworth, Lovelock, Cold Spring, Winnemucca, Golconda, Battle Mountain, Carlin, Elko, Humboldt Wells: the railroad stretched eastward. The survey teams and the graders came first, followed by small flatcars pulled by horses and loaded with ties and rails and fittings. The ties were put down, then the rails and the spikes, two to each tie; finally the fishplates were laid out with bolts and nuts to fasten rail to rail. Now the spikers came hammering the rails to the ties, and then men who adjusted and tightened the fishplates. The rail boss checked and trued the rails, and the ballast crew filled in the bed. When one flatcar was empty, it was tipped off the rails to make room for a loaded one. The process had gone on, mile after mile, through Lake Lahontan, the Humboldt Slough, along the Humboldt River, the northern foothills of the Stillwater Range, up the Humboldt Valley, and to the Tuscarora Mountains. The deserts of Nevada were hot and barren. The sun reflected off alkali, sand, and volcanic ash. Hung Jin had never seen a desert before and he marveled at the strange insects, the lizards, and the small, elusive coyotes that hovered about the campsites. That spring the dry, hard, desert plants bloomed, yellow and red in the monotonous waste. The next winter, the mountains of Nevada received the cold north winds of the Idaho territory, and the laborers walked about shivering in the heavy, cold fogs. Hung Jin bore the hardship with good humor. He had performed his duty to his father and was now busy joining two great oceans together.

At Promontory Point, Utah, Hung Jin rose early, feeling great excitement. For the first day in weeks the weather was clear and the blue skies appeared unreal in their pure color. The bright sun shone down, glinting off the icy puddles which lay about after weeks of rain. The wind blew hard, and the flags which were fastened to telegraph poles snapped all morning.

The meeting place for the eastern and the western railways was a barren plateau high above the Great Salt Lake. With its stunted trees and dried sage brush, it reminded Hung Jin of the plateau beyond his village. The Central Pacific train came first, the balloon stack of its locomotive scarlet and black with bright brass work. Later the Union Pacific train arrived, pulled by a new coal-burning locomotive, its stack tall and straight. Hung Jin thought both locomotives very beautiful and substantial in the brilliant windy day. Their smoke rose and fled, twin trails across the bright sky. Not far from the final rails where the ceremony was to take place, a man sat at a small table on which lay a telegraph key, its wires leading up a nearby pole. Now the bands gathered, the troopers and the celebrities in their fine costumes.

Hung Jin stood by the telegraph operator watching while an official handed him printed messages to transmit. "To everybody. Keep quiet. When the last spike is driven at Promontory Point we will say, 'Done.' Don't break the circuit, but watch for the signals of the blows of the hammer.... Almost ready. Hats off. Prayer is being offered...."

Hung Jin heard little of the prayer except for something about joining the "strength of the Atlantic" with the "love of the Pacific."

The official lay down another card: "We have got done praying, the spike is about to be presented."

As the ceremony continued, Hung Jin felt sadness rise within him. There was something meager and raw and unfinished about the proceedings, as if these men were trying to invent a ritual which would equal the magnificence of their accomplishment. And yet, here they were, a small group of insignificant human beings, shivering in the midst of a desolate plain, the sounds of their speeches and of their bands carried away by the wind. Now Hung Jin thought of those great trees which had fallen to make way for these tracks, he thought of the granite which had been scooped out of the mountains, and the canyons filled with debris, and he thought of the men's lives that had been taken by the task of stretching iron tracks across a continent. The earth had not submitted lightly.

The last spike was placed in a ready-drilled hole and a stout dignitary stepped up holding a maul. With an awkward swing he flailed at the spike and missed it, the maul bouncing off the rail. Hung Jin smiled. The earth was not quite ready to be conquered. After a pause the dignitary lifted the maul again, a few inches from the top of the spike, and tapped it gingerly into the tie.

The operator at Hung Jin's side tapped out three dots and then the word "Done." Hung Jin turned away. There behind the clump of humans and machines lay the gray-brown empty plain. The icy puddles glinted. Several hundred feet away he could make out a dark bird with a broad white stripe down the side of its head. Hung Jin wondered where its fellows were and what this bird thought of this odd gathering. Feeling a sense of sin against the earth, and at the same time, the relief and joy of completion, he walked out on the plateau towards the bird which flew away, displaying now its speckled wings and now its black breast against the sky.

A

B

C

D

E

F

A Laying rails on the Central Pacific Railroad, courtesy of The Bancroft Library, University of California, Berkeley.

B Work on the last mile of the Pacific Railroad, mingling European with Asiatic laborers, sketched by A. R. Waud, courtesy of the Library of Congress.

C Union Pacific train snowbound in a drift near Ogden, from a sketch by J. B. Schultz, courtesy of the Library of Congress.

D Chinese laborer at the laying of the last rail at Promontory, Utah, photograph by A. J. Russell, courtesy of The Oakland Museum, History Department.

E View of Donner Lake from the Sierra Nevada Mountains, with snow sheds, photograph by A. J. Russell, courtesy of The Oakland Museum, History Department.

F An ouzel or dipper (*Cinclus cinclus*).

G Chinese railworker, courtesy of The Bancroft Library, University of California, Berkeley.

G

Acknowledgments

I would like to express my gratitude to the following: my wife, Gloria Kurian Broder, whose sense of fiction and critical eye have improved the book immeasurably, and whose belief in my work has sustained me; Jim and Carolyn Robertson at whose Yolla Bolly Press this project first was born; Jon Beckmann, Wendy Goldwyn, and Jim Cohee, my publisher and editors, whose enthusiasm and critical intelligence have been crucial in bringing the project to completion; my friends of "the canyon," Old Mines Road, and "the floating island," who provided much of the impulse to write about these matters; David Schickele, Leon Seltzer, Nancy Packer, Peter Everwine, and Larry Mohr for helpful advice at the early stages; and my children, Tanya and Adam, who have borne with my efforts with patience and humor.

In my research for this book I owe a special debt to the excellent facilities of the library of the University of California at Berkeley, the files and stacks of which have provided my material. My image gathering was made possible by capable and gracious help from Johann Kooy and his volunteers at the Pictures Collection of the California Academy of the Sciences, Eugene Prince of the Lowie Museum of the University of California, and the staffs of the University Museum of the University of Pennsylvania, the Metropolitan Museum of New York, the Museum of Fine Arts of Boston, the Peabody Museum of Harvard, the Semitic Museum of Harvard, the Museum of Natural History of New York, and the Oakland Museum.

I am indebted to the following institutions for quotations which appear in the text: for the epigraph which begins, "And I saw that . . . ," from *Black Elk Speaks*, by John G. Neihardt, copyright John G. Neihardt, 1932, 1972, published by Simon & Schuster Pocket Books and The University of Nebraska Press, by permission of the John G. Neihardt Trust; for the epigraph which begins, "Then the first wind . . . ," from *Keeping the Night*, by Peter Everwine, excerpted lines from the poem, When God First Said, by Natan Sach as translated by Peter Everwine in collaboration with Shulamith Starkman, by permission of Peter Everwine; for the letter in To Do Earths, which begins, "From Lu-igisa to . . . ," from *Water for Larsa: An Old Babylonian Archive Dealing with Irrigation*, by Stanley D. Walters, copyright Yale University Press, 1970, by permission of Yale University Press; for the prayer in To Do Earths which begins, "O Sin, O Nannar . . . ," excerpted from "Sumero-Akkadian Hymns and Prayers, translated by Ferris J. Stephens on page 386 of *Ancient Near Eastern Texts Relating to the Old Testament*, edited by James B. Pritchard, 3rd edition with Supplement, copyright by Princeton University Press, 1969, by permission of Princeton University Press; for the poem in To Do Earths which begins, "Its canal boat towpaths . . . ," from *The Summerians: Their History, Culture, and Character*, by Samuel Noah Kramer, copyright The University of Chicago, 1963, by permission of The University of Chicago Press; for the prayers in Chernobog's Daughter from *New Larousse Encyclopedia*, edited by Felix Guirard, copyright Paul Hamlyn, 1959, by permission of The Hamlyn Publishing Group Limited.

In choosing the images which follow each tale, I did not attempt to illustrate the events in any literal manner. My choice was dictated rather by a desire to heighten the themes which I was exploring. Therefore I have, now and then, taken liberties with chronology.

The images which illustrate the three part titles are as follows: The Hoop is Planted, an early paleolithic hand axe; The Hoop of Iron, horsehead ornament, Magdalenska gora, Slovenia, Yugoslavia, courtesy of Peabody Museum, Harvard University, photograph by Hillel Burger; The Hoop of Thorns, an early clock movement. The cover image, called an uroboros and appearing also on page 235, is from a 17th century Italian woodcut.